CHERRY AMES, THE MYSTERY IN THE DOCTOR'S OFFICE

TITLES BY HELEN WELLS

CHERRY AMES
THE MYSTERY IN
THE DOCTOR'S
OFFICE

By

HELEN WELLS

SPRINGER PUBLISHING COMPANY

New York

Springer Publishing Company, LLC
11 West 42nd Street
New York, NY 10036-8002
www.springerpub.com

Acquisitions Editor: Sally J. Barhydt
Series Editor: Harriet S. Forman
Production Editor: Carol Cain
Cover design: Mimi Flow
Composition: Apex Publishing, LLC

17   18   /   5

Library of Congress Cataloging-in-Publication Data

Wells, Helen, 1910-
   [Mystery in the doctor's office]
   Cherry Ames, the mystery in the doctor's office / by Helen Wells.
      p. cm.
   Summary: Cherry enjoys being the office nurse for a medical practice in New York City's theater district, although the medical secretary is behaving suspiciously, and spends her weekends helping to fix up a country house belonging to her roommate's family.
   ISBN-13: 978-0-8261-0435-9 (alk. paper)
   ISBN-10: 0-8261-0435-5 (alk. paper)
  [1. Nurses—Fiction. 2. Medical care—Fiction. 3. Dwellings—Maintenance and repair—Fiction. 4. Embezzlement—Fiction. 5. New York (N.Y.)—History—1951—Fiction. 6. Mystery and detective stories.] I. Title.

PZ7.W4644Cjd 2007
[Fic]—dc22

                                            2007035812

Printed in the United States of America by Maple Press

Contents

Foreword

Helen Wells, the author of the Cherry Ames stories, said, "I've always thought of nursing, and perhaps you have, too, as just about the most exciting, important, and rewarding profession there is. Can you think of any other skill that is *always* needed by everybody, everywhere?"

I was and still am a fan of Cherry Ames. Her courageous dedication to her patients; her exciting escapades; her thirst for knowledge; her intelligent application of her nursing skills; and the respect she achieved as a registered nurse (RN) all made it clear to me that I was going to follow in her footsteps and become a nurse—nothing else would do.

Thousands of other young readers were motivated by Cherry Ames to become RNs as well. Through her thought-provoking stories, Cherry Ames led a steady stream of students into schools of nursing across the country well into the 1960s and 1970s when the series ended.

Readers who remember enjoying these books in the past will take pleasure in reading them again now—whether or not they chose nursing as their life's work. Perhaps they will share them with others and even motivate a person or two to choose nursing as their career.

My nursing path has been rich and satisfying. I have delivered babies, cared for people in hospitals and in their homes, and saved lives. I have worked at the bedside and served as an administrator, I have published journals, written articles, taught students, consulted, and given expert testimony. Never once did I regret my decision to become a nurse.

During the time I was publishing a nursing journal, I became acquainted with Robert Wells, brother of Helen Wells. In the course of conversation I learned that Ms. Wells had passed on and left the Cherry Ames copyright to Mr. Wells. Because there is a shortage of nurses here in the US today, I thought, "Why not bring Cherry back to motivate a whole new generation of young people? Why not ask Mr. Wells for the copyright to Cherry Ames?" Mr. Wells agreed, and the republished series is dedicated both to Helen Wells, the original author, and to her brother, Robert Wells, who transferred the rights to me. I am proud to ensure the continuation of Cherry Ames into the twenty-first century.

The final dedication is to you, both new and former readers of Cherry Ames: It is my dream that you enjoy Cherry's nursing skills as well as her escapades. I hope that young readers will feel motivated to choose nursing as their life's work. Remember, as Helen Wells herself said: there's no other skill that's "*always* needed by everybody, everywhere."

Harriet Schulman Forman, RN, EdD
Series Editor

CHERRY AMES, THE MYSTERY
IN THE DOCTOR'S OFFICE

CHAPTER I

To Dr. Fairall's

〜〜〜〜〜〜〜〜〜〜〜〜〜〜〜〜〜〜〜〜〜〜〜〜〜〜〜〜〜〜

"SPECIAL-DELIVERY LETTER!" THE MAILMAN CALLED. HE rang the Spencer Club's doorbell, loud and long.

It was seven o'clock Monday morning. Inside the little Greenwich Village apartment, one and then another alarm clock shrilled. Four young nurses in the closet-size bedrooms squirmed and struggled to wake up. Cherry groped for her robe, stepped over Gwen's pillow on the floor, and staggered to the front door.

As she opened it, the mailman sang out, " 'Morning! Lovely warm day."

Cherry noticed the mailman was looking at her feet, so she looked down, too. She discovered she was barefoot. She tossed back her dark hair and said with dignity:

"Good morning. I'll accept the letter. Thank you. OK, it's for Miss Gwen Jones."

She felt relieved that the letter was not for her. Not a summons to come home to Hilton, Illinois, just when she was about to start on a challenging new job as office nurse for Dr. Fairall.

"You're welcome," said the mailman. "It's from Canton, Ohio. Fat letter, something's enclosed. Hope I didn't disturb anybody this early."

Cherry smiled. "Who wakes *you*, Mr. Mailman?"

"My wife. And the cat wakes *her*, because the cat wants its breakfast. Well, so long, now."

The mailman left. Cherry closed the door.

Josie Franklin, in her rather squeaky voice, said, "So, indirectly, we've been awakened by a cat. That's all right. I like cats."

"Where's my letter?" asked Gwen. She was in pajamas, her freckled face dripping water. "Didn't the mailman or somebody say Jones?"

Cherry put the special-delivery letter in Gwen's wet hand, and as she turned to go to her bedroom, collided with Bertha Larsen who was just coming into the living room. Bertha was a big, fair, hearty girl from Minnesota farm country. Her patients often said they felt better just looking at her.

"Good morning to all!" said Bertha. "Cherry has a fine day to start at Dr. Fairall's." Over her robe Bertha tied an apron around her ample figure. "It's my turn to get the first shower after breakfast this morning."

"Aren't you going to open that letter and tell us what's in it?" Josie asked Gwen.

"Feels as if there are snapshots in it," Gwen mumbled. "Where's a letter opener—or a knife—? Gosh, I'd better get dressed first, or I'll be late reporting for duty."

Cherry was halfway down the hall, heading for the shower, but she had heard Bertha, and called, "I'll fix breakfast and shower last, Bertha. It's only fair—since I just swelled the ranks from three to four."

"You go get ready for your new job," Bertha answered affectionately, and edged sideways into the tiny kitchenette. "Whew, it's a hot morning. Even so early."

In the nurses' scramble to get to their four jobs on time, Josie offered plaintively, "I could read the letter aloud to you, Gwen, while you dress. Or at breakfast."

"How do you know it isn't a love letter?" Gwen teased.

"Any letter from your aunt in Canton, Ohio, can't be *that* private. Oh, dear!" Josie wailed from her closet. "Where's my clean slip?"

Cherry smiled to herself at the familiar bedlam. During the week Gwen rushed off to her private duty case, Josie Franklin reported for general duty nursing at a small hospital, and Bertha to a clinic. Cherry could remember times when the other four members of the Spencer Club had been here, too—Why, today's confusion was nothing!

Yesterday and the day before—Memorial Day weekend—the Spencer Club had indulged in late, leisurely breakfasts. Then they had caught up with news of one another's jobs, beaux, families, clothes. This weekend they had concentrated on Cherry Ames, who had arrived earlier in the week—either as a temporary guest, or as a fairly permanent resident. That is, Cherry had come to New York for a job interview.

She had come feeling uncertain whether she was ready for another job right away, after her strenuous nursing work in Africa, in a jungle hospital. Although she had rested at home in Illinois and visited with her family, her mother wanted her to rest still longer. Her father frankly didn't want her to go away—"Can't you go back to your staff nurse job at Hilton Hospital, Cherry?" But by now her old job was filled. Cherry's twin brother, Charlie, had mediated.

"I know how Cherry feels—it's no good having nothing to do." He was an aviation engineer, now home on vacation from his job in Southern California. Charlie suggested Cherry might find some nursing work that was not too taxing—"Since she isn't happy unless she is nursing."

When the Spencer Club phoned Cherry about Dr. Fairall and his two associate doctors needing an office nurse, that position sounded just right. Last week Cherry had had an interview with Dr. William Fairall. By Friday she was able to tell the Spencer Club: "You're going to be stuck with me for a while. Dr. Fairall has hired me."

The only drawback, Cherry thought, was having to spend the summer in the city. She loved New York, but she would miss her small town's trees, gardens, and her father's backyard barbecues.

Gwen said, as they finished dressing, "You know, Cherry, I hear that that young Dr. Grey Russell in Dr. Fairall's office is terribly attractive."

Cherry's dark eyes sparkled. "It's the third or fourth time you've told me that valuable piece of information. Have you met him?"

"Once or twice," Gwen replied. "I hope you'll like working with him and the others."

"I expect to like everybody at my new job," Cherry said. "Or at least I'll try to get along amiably."

"Breakfast!" Bertha called. "Ready or not, come!"

Breakfast was hasty. In self-defense, or so she said, Gwen opened the letter at the table and scanned it.

"Very bad manners to read letters at the table," said Josie.

"Just for that I won't tell you what's in it—until we all come home tonight," Gwen said. She read on. "Say! This is wonderful! In case any of us wants a summer house on Long Island, we may borrow my aunt's."

"Well! Very nice! Near enough to commute?" Bertha asked.

"Has it a garden?" Cherry asked. "Or is it near a beach, by any good luck?"

"Yes, to all those things. Sort of yes. Oh—oh—" Gwen turned a handwritten page and frowned as she read. "Aunt Bess says there's a catch to her offer. Nothing we couldn't cope with—if we—hmm—" Gwen stared into space. "Think of the swimming parties we could have—lots of guests—picnics afterward at our very own house!"

Cherry gently tapped Gwen's freckled hand. "Come down off that cloud. Look at the time!"

Bertha looked at the clock. "I'll never get a shower! Josie, your turn to be the dishwasher. Excuse me." Bertha ran.

"I'll help you," Cherry offered.

Josie nodded her thanks, then asked Gwen, "What's the catch in your Aunt Bess's offer? Aren't you going to show us the snapshots she sent of the place?"

"This evening," Gwen said firmly. "And it's a good, solid cloud." She went to the grocery store, then to the garage to get her car.

By the time Gwen returned, everyone was ready to go. They put away the groceries and propped the letter on the mantel. Then they piled into Gwen's car—a middle-aged car, but it ran.

Cherry was the first to be let out, when they reached the Broadway theater district. Her friends wished her good luck.

Gwen said, "You'll have a lively time, what with Dr. Fairall's show-business patients! 'Bye!"

Cherry left Broadway and walked west on one of the side streets in the Fifties. She passed theater after theater, television studios, casting offices, costumers' shops, wigmakers, hotels, window displays of musical instruments, pawnshops, restaurants, rehearsal lofts. In broad daylight the district and its people looked hard working and rather shabby. Where was the magic and beauty of the theater at eight-thirty A.M.?

When she walked past the famous old hospital that served this area, Cherry came back with a start from make-believe to the real world. Dr. Fairall was affiliated with this hospital. There he had treated actors, singers, dancers, and stagehands who became part of his practice. He had other, less colorful patients, too.

Or so Gwen had said. She had obtained her information from her own employer, Dr. Merriam, who was an old friend of Bill Fairall's. In fact, Dr. Merriam had recommended Cherry, knowing her work from the time she had been a companion nurse to one of his patients. It was in Dr. Merriam's office that Cherry's interview with Dr. Fairall had taken place last week. They had met there since Dr. Fairall was pressed for time, and was on his way to a medical consultation.

Cherry had had an impression of a vigorous, hardworking, zestful man. His warm concern for his patients came first. He worked at medical research, enjoyed the theater, tennis, hunting, fishing, and found time for family and friends and even some community work. No wonder this busy man had said to Cherry:

"I rely on my staff, Miss Ames, to do what needs doing—apart from purely medical matters. I don't have time to spell out instructions for every administrative or business detail. So, you see, running that office would be largely up to you! And to my excellent medical secretary and my laboratory technician—you'd work with them as a team. We have a part-time R.N. who comes in occasionally for a few hours, but the main responsibility would be yours. Think you can do it?"

Cherry thought she could. She'd certainly try to do her very best.

Ahead, a few blocks away, Cherry could see the broad, blue Hudson River. Dr. Fairall's house must be right here, in this residential block. There it was—a Victorian brownstone—with a scrubbed flagstone entrance yard, freshly painted white shutters and Venetian blinds, the doctors' nameplates on the door.

Cherry knew that the brownstone's first two floors had been converted into medical offices. The two top floors, Cherry understood, each held an apartment that Dr. Fairall rented to private tenants. The top-floor apartment looked vacant. At least, the windows up there were bare.

Cherry rang the doctors' doorbell, then walked in. Though it was early, two men and a woman with a small boy waited in the reception room. Cherry's practiced eye noticed the child's pallor and crankiness—convalescing, probably. The two men, reading newspapers, looked well and well taken care of, though one man looked awfully cross.

"How much longer to wait? I'm due at my office," he complained to the woman in white uniform.

She sat behind a desk, sorting mail. The woman was dignified, with sharp features and fastidious movements. Her graying blond hair gleamed with cleanliness and was combed smooth as a cap. Her hands were beautifully kept, as a lady's hands should be. She held herself erect, head high, as if she thought of herself as someone rather special.

"I'm really sorry, Mr. Babcock." The woman's voice was soothingly low-pitched. "Dr. Fairall sometimes gets delayed in traffic. He should be here any minute now. And you are his first patient this morning."

The patient was placated, and reopened his newspaper. The woman looked at Cherry, smiled, and her agreeable, rather reserved glance took in every last detail about Cherry.

"You must be our new nurse?" she said in a lowered voice. "Dr. Fairall has told me about you, Miss Ames. Hello and welcome. I'm Irene Wick, the doctor's medical secretary."

"How do you do, Miss Wick?" said Cherry, and smiled back. "It's nice to meet you." She kept her voice low, too, in the patients' presence. "I hope I'm not late."

"You're in plenty of time. It's just that I'm early—the first one to come in the mornings, the last one to leave at night."

Her words had a disturbing ring—was she boasting? or scared? or on the defensive? A graduate nurse outranked all others on a physician's office staff. Cherry realized the woman might be worried about having to get along with a new, unknown nurse—someone much younger than herself.

Cherry tried to reassure her. "You're very conscientious," she said. "Dr. Fairall told me you're expert at managing his office. You'll have to break me in, I'm afraid."

The medical secretary relaxed. "Of course. I'll be happy to help you get started. By the way, it's *Mrs.* Wick."

She motioned Cherry to come into her work area, which was simply an open end of the reception room, with a huge desk holding telephones and appointment books, and a typewriter. Two small chairs and file cabinets were placed against the wall. Beyond was a closed door that, Mrs. Wick murmured, led into Dr. Fairall's office.

She pressed a button on the intercom and said, "Dottie, our new nurse is here. I'd like to take her on the grand tour. Can you come meet Miss Ames and pinch-hit for me?"

Both telephones rang. Mrs. Wick answered and quickly made appointments for patients. The laboratory technician came in, a tall rugged girl wearing an unbuttoned long white lab coat flapping over her dress, and an elaborate hairdo. Though she appeared at first glance to be sophisticated, Cherry looked beyond the hairdo and saw an ill-at-ease, uncertain young woman. She seemed a little intimidated by Irene Wick, who said crisply:

"Miss Ames, this is Dottie Nash, our lab technician." The medical secretary opened the door into Dr. Fairall's handsome office, leaving the door ajar, and motioned the other two to come in. Here they could talk privately for a minute. "With three physicians here," Irene Wick said to Cherry, "we run a great many lab tests, too many to send out daily to a commercial lab. Whenever Dottie isn't busy in her lab, she answers phones, makes appointments, acts as receptionist, and—and—"

"Take patients' payments and run errands for our doctors," Dottie interrupted, then looked self-conscious.

Mrs. Wick laughed softly, adding, "And dusts the reception room when I haven't time, or when Winnie our cleaner has skipped over some dust—and Dottie helps me with typing the patients' histories. Miss Ames, there's a great deal to do here, and such a rush, usually! We all pitch in and do a little of everything. Whoever is around when a phone rings, answers it. Whenever a patient is ready to pay for his visit or treatment, whoever is around accepts the payments. We don't *intend* for our jobs to overlap, but—" Irene Wick shrugged, and, for all her cool dignity, a laugh bubbled out of her. "Honestly, we run! Even when our part-time R.N. is here—Mrs. Jackson won't be in today, incidentally."

Cherry smiled. "Dr. Fairall told me his staff works as a team, and I do want to cooperate. The only thing is, I must be sure to take care of the nursing duties *first*. First and adequately."

"Of course," Irene Wick said, and Dottie Nash nodded, examining a fingernail.

A telephone rang, a buzzer sounded—apparently from one of the doctors' offices—and a baby cried in the reception room. Dottie Nash muttered, "S'cuse me," and hurried off.

"We'll make our tour as quickly as possible," Irene Wick said to Cherry. She led her through Dr. Fairall's office to a side door and into a hall.

"Do any of the doctors here treat infants?" Cherry asked curiously. In a city of any size, doctors specialized; pediatricians treated infants and young children. A baby here? Cherry knew that Dr. Fairall was a general practitioner, that Dr. Earl Lamb treated older persons (she'd heard he was elderly himself), and that Dr. Grey Russell was an internist, that is primarily a diagnostician. The youngest doctor made house calls, and handled night and weekend emergencies for the other two physicians. The faint sound of the baby crying made Cherry wonder if Dr. Fairall's practice included infants. She asked Mrs. Wick.

"No, Dr. Fairall doesn't accept any patients under the age of thirteen," the medical secretary said. "Of course he or Dr. Russell would take care of anyone in an emergency. The baby's mother is our patient. Dr. Fairall is watching her for a tendency to diabetes. Now, along this hall, Miss Ames—"

~~~~~~

CHAPTER II

Getting Acquainted

CHERRY AND MRS. WICK STARTED OFF ON THE GET-acquainted tour.

The doctors' house was long and narrow, and so was the hall. Doors lined all of one side of it. But first, before starting down the hall, Mrs. Wick showed Cherry two facilities. Opposite the side door of Dr. Fairall's office, tucked under the staircase, was a small lavatory. Next to it was a walk-in closet with a sterilizer, clean linens, supplies of cotton, gauze, wooden swabs. Medicines were kept in a locked cabinet.

"Here is the nurse's key." Mrs. Wick reached into her uniform pocket for a key ring. She removed two keys. "And here is the key to the house—to the front door, Miss Ames. Each of us has these door keys, in case someone is out sick or delayed, or if there's an emergency."

"Thank you." Cherry put the two keys in her purse. Irene Wick certainly seemed to be in charge here. "Have you been with Dr. Fairall long?"

"About two years. Dottie Nash has been here a year. I—No, I won't say I hired her, but I did find her for the doctor. I sifted out the other applicants' letters telling their qualifications."

Cherry wondered if the three physicians left absolutely everything in her charge. Apparently they did rely on Mrs. Wick. Well, she must have proved herself capable and worthy of her position of trust.

"Now, here is our big examining room." Mrs. Wick led Cherry down the hall to a room next door to Dr. Fairall's office. Mrs. Wick opened the door to show Cherry. "Electrocardiograph, P.BI., and fluoroscope in here." P.B.I. stood for Protein Bound Iodine; it was used to estimate the thyroid protein in the blood—the thyroid having control over many body functions. P.B.I. was used more than the basal metabolism machine, because it was considered more accurate.

"Who left the small sterilizer plugged in?" the medical secretary grumbled. She unplugged it. "Doctors can be so forgetful—so preoccupied with their work." She tested an empty syringe to make sure it was working. "I must remember to order a syringe Dr. Lamb asked for. And more cotton. Will you need any special supplies, Miss Ames?"

"Thanks. But let's wait until Dr. Fairall talks to me today, and gives me some direction."

Irene Wick looked at her so coldly that Cherry felt disturbed. Had she said something that offended the medical secretary? Cherry wondered. What a contradictory woman Mrs. Wick was! Obliging at one moment, hostile the next.

They continued down the hall to two small examining rooms, each equipped with a scale, a table with a thermometer, stethoscope, and a few simple instruments, and a high examining table.

At the very end of the hall was the laboratory, with the usual tables full of test tubes in racks, Bunsen burners, Petri dishes containing test cultures, charts and notes, a small refrigerator, and tall stools and a supply closet.

"I could shake Dottie Nash sometimes," the medical secretary said, "for some of her careless ways—her mind is on clothes and dances when she's doing *any* task except her lab work. The lab seems to fascinate her. Our three doctors say she's a first-rate technician."

"Good for her," Cherry said. "It's key work."

A laboratory technician, or medical technologist, performs biochemical tests of the patients' blood and other body fluids. With the help of these results, the physicians can recognize and accurately diagnose an illness—and so can prescribe the right medication and treatment.

The lab was sunny and pleasant. This room, originally the kitchen, looked out on a backyard with tall grass, a leafy fruit tree, and some feasting sparrows. Cherry noticed the back door was open, and remarked on it.

"Grey—Dr. Russell—may be out there for a few minutes," Irene Wick said. "I shouldn't call him by his first name, should I? But he seems so young to me— just recently started to practice." Mrs. Wick smiled at Cherry. "You're young, too." She stepped outdoors and motioned Cherry to follow.

A sturdy young man in a white cotton coat was standing with his hands in his pockets, staring at the ground. He was thinking hard, and though he saw the two women, he took another few seconds to finish his thought and write down a note before looking directly at them. Then he said, "Hello."

Mrs. Wick said, "Are we interrupting you, Doctor?"

"Not at all. Figuring a possible new angle on the Miller case. I'll need the case record and lab report, please. And the Cox case history."

"Right away," Mrs. Wick said. "Dr. Russell, this is Miss Cherry Ames, our new full-time nurse."

"Oh, yes, Dr. Fairall told me about you." He shook hands cordially with Cherry. "Awfully glad you're here."

Cherry thought he looked boyish with his fresh, fair coloring and easy way of moving. But his quiet manner and calm blue-gray eyes were serious. Cherry said, "I hope I can be of help here." For though most of her work would be with Dr. Fairall, she would do some nursing work with the younger doctor and older doctor as needed.

Dr. Grey Russell asked a little awkwardly whether his appointment had come in yet.

"No, he's not due yet," the secretary said.

"My first patient canceled at the last minute, Miss Ames," young Dr. Russell said, "that's how I happen to be out here. Out of the air conditioning. Built in, can't turn it off, can't open windows. It's unnatural, I don't like it. And I'll be indoors here until four this afternoon. Then hospital rounds. Then house calls. Mrs. Wick understands, but I don't want *you* to think that I see my patients under this tree."

They all exchanged smiles, and agreed that Dr. Russell would show Miss Ames the second floor, while Mrs. Wick returned to her work.

Grey Russell was nice, Cherry thought. He was more comfortable and sympathetic to be with than Mrs. Wick. He led Cherry back along the hall and showed her the small self-service elevator at the front of the house. Usually he ran up and down the stairs, he said, rather than wait for the elevator. They rode up this time. On the second floor he showed Cherry another row of rooms along a long hall.

First, facing the street, was a large treatment room. Here medications, injections, dressings were administered. Here, too, was equipment for allergy tests. Grey Russell and Cherry walked through to the next room. This main supply room held a tremendous, well-stocked closet, shelves of linen coats, towels, sheets, a sink, and another big sterilizer, with a tray of rubber gloves and disinfectants beside it.

"Now we come to Dr. Lamb's office—brace yourself," the young doctor said with a grin. "He's a little bit eccentric—won't let the girls straighten up his office, and they have to dust it secretly. But he's an excellent doctor."

Dr. Earl Lamb was not in yet—his hours were eleven to three—so they ventured to open his door. His office was chaos. Medications, papers, instruments were scattered all over the room.

Cherry gasped. "How does he ever find anything?"

"He does. And his patients are devoted to him. He calls his eighty-year-old patients 'my little girls and boys.'" Grey Russell chuckled and closed the door. "He may or may not come in today; he's too elderly to work every day. But when you meet him, you'll see he's extraordinarily gifted."

Next door was a small examining room. Then came a small treatment room containing an infrared lamp. Still farther down the hall was a dressing room for the feminine members of the staff. Grey Russell knocked, then invited Cherry to look in.

"You'll find a desk for your use in there," he said.

She saw a sketchily furnished room with a desk, a couch, a few wooden chairs, and a clothes rack. After glancing in at the second small examining room on this floor, they came to young Dr. Russell's office. It was directly above the lab, with windows looking down on the green backyard.

Grey Russell's office was in meticulous order. On the bookshelves he had medical reference books. Noticing Cherry's interest in his books, he said:

"Some of those volumes are textbooks I used in medical school. Some are even newer works. Dr. Fairall gave me some of them. He certainly keeps abreast of medical discoveries."

"You sound happy, Dr. Russell, about being associated with Dr. Fairall," Cherry said.

"Yes, I am happy—and lucky, too. He's giving me my start. He's known me since I was an intern, and he lectured to us—and he liked my work. So when I was ready to start practice, he invited me to be his relief man."

Cherry said, "He must respect you, to be willing to entrust his patients to you."

Grey Russell looked faintly embarrassed. "He lets me have this office at a nominal rent, until my own practice grows, and I can afford my own place. Or maybe he'll want me to stay on here, if he ever decides to stop working so hard. Bill Fairall does the work of three men—"

"Speaking of work," Cherry murmured, "I'm afraid I'm keeping you."

"Not at all. It helps to get acquainted, if we're going to work together." The young man walked over to his desk and picked up some case records. "The quick Mrs. Wick—never have to ask her twice for anything. By the way, Miss Cherry Ames, where have you done most of your nursing?"

"Oh, various places. But mostly in my own Middle West. Illinois."

"I thought I heard a Midwest twang in your voice. And those rosy cheeks couldn't belong to a city girl—unless it's rouge."

"It's not rouge, Doctor; it's the result of fresh air and a hearty appetite," Cherry said, laughing a little. "Are you a country boy?"

"Upstate New York." He named one of the smaller cities. "Vineyards, lakes, farms—and steel plants. Speaking of a hearty appetite, I'll challenge you to an eating contest sometime after a hard day's work. We'll—"

A voice announced from an intercom box: "Dr. Russell, your appointment is here."

He pressed a button and answered, "Please send Mr. Wilson up." Then to Cherry, "If Dr. Fairall doesn't need you immediately, I could use your help in changing a dressing. Broken hand, transplanted tendon—it's pretty painful for the patient. The poor man fell, and tried to break his fall with his outstretched hand. Let me know on the intercom how soon you can be back here, please."

"Yes, Doctor," Cherry said, and left his office thinking about this patient. Goodbye for the time being to an eating contest. It didn't sound at all romantic, but it might be fun! Cherry sped down the hall and—just as Dr. Grey Russell had predicted—ran down the stairs rather than wait for the elevator.

She found that Dr. Fairall was in, and would let her know when he needed her. Cherry changed quickly into her white uniform. She worked with Grey Russell on Mr. Wilson's artfully reconstructed hand—worked with admiration for Dr. Fairall who had done the surgery and for the silent, concentrating young doctor.

That first day at Dr. Fairall's Cherry mostly just got acquainted. She had a whirlwind interview with Dr. Fairall, assisted him in examining and testing a variety of patients, read some patients' medical histories at his request, and in general learned how the office was run. Dr. Earl Lamb did not come in; neither did the part-time nurse. Everyone—Dr. Fairall, Dr. Grey Russell, Mrs. Wick, Dottie Nash—did his best to help their new R.N.

By the end of the day Cherry was thoroughly interested in her new job. The Spencer Club wanted to hear all about it, and Cherry told them at supper that evening.

Even so, interested as the nurses were, Cherry saw their attention wander to the letter on the mantel. Josie Franklin, in particular, kept eyeing it, until Cherry exclaimed:

"Oh, I can't wait any longer, either! Gwen, won't you give up your iron restraint and *read it*?"

Gwen silently read a page of her aunt's letter. Meanwhile, she handed the girls several color snapshots. These showed a rambling, roomy cottage, surrounded by shady lawns and flower gardens.

"How can Gwen's aunt and uncle bear not to use this place themselves?" Bertha exclaimed. And Josie said, "Are we ever lucky!"

"Ahem!" said Gwen. "Listen to this!" She read aloud from the letter:

"'This is the place where you used to visit us, Gwen. You remember, it is near a beach with surf swimming.

In another direction is that protected bay for sailing.'"
Gwen stopped reading to say that the house was in a
pretty Long Island village, with a few stores, and a fas-
cinating swap shop that was run for the benefit of the
local church. She read again from the letter:

"'Your uncle and I haven't been able to come East to
use the house for several summers, and according to a
letter from a village neighbor—unfortunately—'"

Gwen groaned, then scowled, as she scanned the
rest of the letter. Pained cries arose from her three
curious listeners.

"All right, all right, I'll read you the awful part of
it," Gwen quieted them. "And I quote: 'The house had
been sublet, partially furnished, then stood vacant. We
don't want to sell it because your uncle was born in this
house, and he is sentimental about it. Maybe someday
we will use it for a retirement place. Our neighbors
report that the place is in sad disrepair, and will need
a lot of work to make it livable again. The grounds are
overgrown. The barn—'"

"So there's a barn, too!" said Bertha.

"'—needs a coat of paint. The old well should be
cleaned out. Anyway—'" Here Gwen fell silent again,
to the exasperation of Cherry, Josie, and Bertha.

"Anyway, *what?*" they demanded.

"'Anyway,'" Gwen read aloud, uncertainty in her
freckled face, "'if you and your nurse friends feel ambitious enough to put some hard work into the house and
grounds, the place is yours to use for many years to
come. Should you decide to go ahead, your uncle says

just to send him the bills for all repairs and expenses like new window glass, paint, grass seed, plumbing, and so on.'" Murmurs of relief and appreciation greeted this fiscal news. Gwen broke into giggles, and read further:

"'Your uncle also says I am a wretch to mention this dilapidated house to you girls at all, what with the hard work entailed. He strongly advises you to spend your spare time this summer quietly and restfully in an air-conditioned movie house. With best love from us both, and please don't send me any more chocolate butter creams from New York. I enjoy them but am getting too plump. Love, Aunt Bess.

"'P.S. The enclosed photographs were taken several years ago. It *was* a lovely place, once.'"

The four girls looked at one another. Cherry said, "I'll bet we could make the place lovely again."

Bertha was cautious. "First, we should drive out and take a look at the place. Then we should figure carefully how much work, how much time, we'd have to invest. Remember, we are free only on weekends. Maybe it would not be possible."

Josie said it was too bad that the other members of the Spencer Club were away—Vivian Warren, working for a surgeon out West; Mai Lee, taking the summer off to rest and visit with her family in San Francisco; Marie Swift, on a private duty case in Boston. Ann Evans was still in Canada with her husband. "If all eight of us were here," Josie said, "we could surely fix up the place."

"We'll ask our friends to help us," Gwen said. "We'll invite anyone we know for swimming-and-picnicking-and-working weekends."

"We-ll," Cherry started. But Gwen's suggestion could be discussed later. The first thing to do was act on Bertha's sound advice. "How soon can we see the place?"

Next weekend was the soonest time.

"Well, we'll *aim* for next weekend. Anyway, it's wonderful of Gwen's aunt and uncle to make this offer," Cherry said.

CHAPTER III

Parade of Patients

"—AN ACCIDENT AT LAST EVENING'S BALLET PERFOR-mance," the newscaster was saying as Cherry switched on the radio in Gwen's car. It was Thursday, a fine June morning, and the four nurses were on their way to work.

"A member of the ballet company, Miss Leslie Crewe, who has been a ballet dancer since the age of thirteen, leaped and then fell or fainted—"

"What?" Cherry turned around to Josie.

"I said, 'Louder, please!'" Josie shouted over the traffic noise. Cherry obliged.

"When she fell, three men dancers carried her off stage gracefully. Most of the audience was not aware that the Silver Princess, Miss Crewe's role in the ballet, should pirouette and whirl off the stage. The three men harlequins then reappeared on stage, resuming their places in the ensemble. Miss Crewe was treated backstage by the house doctor, and by her own physician who was in the audience. At first it was rumored that the Silver Princess had broken her leg, but the ballet company's press agent denied this. Dr. William Fairall took—"

Bertha in great excitement tapped Cherry on the shoulder. "*Your* doctor! You hear that?"

Cherry nodded, trying to hear as a Broadway bus rumbled alongside.

"The young dancer was taken to the hospital by ambulance, where she would stay overnight. Dr. Fairall promised a bulletin today on Leslie Crewe's condition.

"Elsewhere in New York, three police horses found that Central Park can be cool, cooler than—"

Gwen switched the radio off. She nosed the car toward the curb and announced, "First stop for our glamour nurse, specializing today in ballet dancers!"

Cherry climbed out and waved goodbye to her friends, then practically ran to Dr. Fairall's street. For the sake of dignity, she tried to hold her pace down to a fast trot. But curiosity about Leslie whisked her along.

Dr. Fairall was already in his office, doors left wide open, speaking cheerfully into his telephone. Cherry was surprised to see him there so early, but apparently Dr. Fairall's hours and plans were fluid and open to last-minute changes, as his patients required. The medical secretary, who was taking off her hat, whispered to Cherry, "Doctor is holding a press interview on the phone. Strict orders—no reporters are ever allowed to come here. We'd be swamped!"

"You can tell your readers that Leslie Crewe hasn't broken any bones!" Dr. Fairall reported. "She isn't even badly bruised—a dancer knows how to fall. She collapsed. Not an accident, a collapse."

Dr. Fairall listened, cocking his handsome massive head. He saw Cherry and smiled at her.

"Well, she started dancing again too soon after little H.J. was born, and—worse—she dieted." Cherry knew that some girls grow plump after having a baby. "Overdid the dieting. Malnutrition. And overexertion.... You're welcome.... 'Bye." Dr. Fairall hung up.

His phone instantly rang again. He repeated the same information, then hung up. Meanwhile, Irene Wick went upstairs to change into uniform.

Dr. Fairall restlessly walked into the empty reception room.

"I'm worried about those two youngsters, Cherry," Dr. Fairall said. Bill Fairall, breezy and friendly, had put her on a first-name basis right away. "What'll the kids do? Here's Leslie, unable to dance for weeks to come. And Henry J., Henry Young, her husband—he's a talented young actor—but the play he is in closes this week. Both kids are out of work. He has half a promise for a job—late this summer. Can't eat promises. Or pay the rent with promises, can you? And there's little H.J.—I brought that young fellow into the world six months ago."

Dr. Fairall threw himself into a chair. He sat and thought in silence. A phone rang. Cherry answered and made an appointment for a patient with Dr. Lamb.

Then, after looking at today's appointments for Dr. Fairall, she drew from the files the case histories and charts of the patients who were coming that day.

"You know, Leslie sent my wife and me tickets for last evening's performance," Dr. Fairall said musingly. "A good thing I was on hand to help. Now what do Henry J. and Leslie do if he can't find a job right away? Any old job, so long as it pays. It takes time to find work." Henry J. had admitted to him last night at the hospital that they had no money except their salaries. Having the baby had eaten up their small savings.

"Well, Dr. Fairall," Cherry asked, "don't your ballet dancer and actor have families who might tide them over during this emergency?"

Dr. Fairall explained that their families lived out of town, and could not give any help, unless Henry J. and Leslie and the baby wanted to move into one or the other parents' house.

"Golly, these kids wouldn't go running home for help. Too spunky for that. Too ambitious." Dr. Fairall told Cherry that both Leslie and Henry J. had come to New York in spite of their parents' disapproval—"or let's say *very* faint enthusiasm"—for careers in the theater. Separately, then together, Leslie and Henry J. made their own way.

"They had some rough times—as you can imagine, Cherry. Having a baby to care for makes this current emergency even harder, of course. Hmm. Well, maybe I could—"

He stood up, rubbed his nose, and marched vigorously into his office. "Cherry!" He instructed her to set up the treatment and examining rooms, before changing into her white uniform.

Cherry felt odd working in her street clothes—a yellow linen dress. At eight A.M. Mr. Forsythe was due for some tests before going to his office. Mr. Gatti was coming in at eight-thirty for Dr. Fairall to look at an infected finger, which he was treating. And at nine A.M.—arranged by the doctor's around-the-clock telephone answering service—Mrs. Lance wanted an infrared treatment to ease acute arthritic pains in her right arm. Other patients with appointments later in the day were several women, three older men, and a student to be vaccinated for a passport.

Cherry scanned the recent entries on the Forsythe, Gatti, and Lance case records. What would be needed? Nothing special for Forsythe or Lance—medication and a sterile dressing for Gatti. Vaccine for the traveling student—she'd get that when needed.

As Cherry scampered to gather supplies, young Dr. Grey Russell came in. He gave her a quiet smile, helped himself to some antitoxin serum from the supply closet under the stairs, and kept right on going.

"Emergency," he said. Cherry followed him and stood listening as he started up the staircase. "If Mrs. Jackson"—the part-time R.N.—"isn't here by eleven, or if Dr. Lamb needs her at eleven, will you work with me? Jeannie Adams, she's fourteen, thinks she pulled or tore a ligament in her shoulder."

"Certainly, Dr. Russell," Cherry said.

"Grey to you." But not in front of patients, of course. "Tell Irene to send the injured construction workman up to me right away. On the elevator—don't let him climb the stairs. Thanks."

Cherry went to answer a ringing telephone at the reception desk. Irene Wick came in, dressed all in white. Courteous and firm, she relieved Cherry of the call. Phones rang again—it was usually this busy every morning, sometimes all day long. When the phones were quiet for a few minutes, Cherry delivered Dr. Grey Russell's message about the workman.

"Yes, I'll watch for the workman," Irene Wick said. "About the telephone calls, Cherry—it's terribly kind of you to dash to the phones. But when I'm around, *especially* before or after the patients come in, in force— Well, I'm sure you have more important things to do than answer phones. Just call me to the phone, my dear."

Cherry was puzzled. This statement—or request?— contradicted what Mrs. Wick had said on Cherry's first day here, about their jobs overlapping. Then Cherry remembered an incident that had occurred late yesterday afternoon. She said in embarrassment:

"I'm sorry if I intruded on a personal phone conversation of yours. When I picked up an extension phone yesterday at five-thirty, I didn't realize—"

There were three phones, three extensions, and an intercom system.

"It wasn't at all personal," Mrs. Wick interrupted crisply. "Just a patient who enjoys grumbling to me. And incidentally, Cherry, you really needn't stay so late." Irene Wick smiled indulgently at her, but Cherry thought the woman's eyes were cold. "*I* have to be here, anyway, Cherry, to run the office, so you needn't be stuck, late *or* early."

Cherry murmured, "Thank you very much, hut it'll depend on how my work goes each day."

This was the second time the medical secretary had made it obvious she wanted to be first to arrive and last to leave. Why?

Cherry remembered how wary the man on the phone had sounded yesterday when she, not Irene, answered. And how Irene, picking up another extension, had sharply told Cherry to hang up.

"If you want to run upstairs and change into uniform," the medical secretary offered, "I'll tell Mr. Forsythe you'll be right with him, to start some of the tests."

"Oh, thanks, I'll be quick," Cherry said.

She started for either the stairs or elevator. The elevator door was just opening. A man and woman stepped out and collided with Cherry.

"Awfully sorry." The middle-aged couple backed off to make room for Cherry, just as the street door opened. A messenger boy burst in like a rocket, and collided with them. They ricocheted back on Cherry.

"Oh, my! Sorry, young lady!" the man said.

"Where do I deliver this?" The messenger held up a large, plain white unaddressed envelope. "Where'll I find Mrs. Irene Tick?"

"My dear girl, we've battered you!" said the woman.

"Wick, not Tick," Cherry gasped. "In there." To the couple, she said, "Not at all, Mrs.—ah, not battered at all."

"Our name is Davis," the man said. "We're Dr. Fairall's tenants on the third floor."

The Davises smiled, held the elevator door for her, and disappeared—as the messenger tore off in the wrong direction, down the hall. Cherry noticed him too late—the elevator door closed automatically. Up she went.

It was only later, while Cherry was taking an electrocardiogram of plump, pink Mr. Forsythe's heart, that the incident crossed her mind. Why was a letter to Mrs. Wick sent by messenger, instead of mailed? Why was the envelope blank? But this was no time to wonder. Cherry paid attention to the graph slowly issuing from the electrocardiogram machine as Mr. Forsythe breathed.

"Looks good," Dr. Fairall said when Cherry brought the graph to him at his desk. "Tell Mr. Forsythe I'll see him now. He's in good shape, but I want to impress on him not to gain any more weight."

"He looks like a kewpie, you know," Cherry said, and Dr. Fairall grinned.

Dottie Nash had run the basal metabolism test for Mr. Forsythe. Dr. Fairall operated the fluoroscope himself.

Cherry did an electrocardiogram for a patient of Dr. Lamb—and so met that elderly gentleman for the first time. She understood on seeing him why Dr. Lamb worked only a few days a week. He was a very old man, thin and brittle, pink-faced, with heavily veined hands and hair like sparse white silk. Yet he was surprisingly quick and dapper. His tired eyes still sparkled, and his pointed nose reminded Cherry of an inquisitive chipmunk's. He would not wear the usual white cotton coat.

"I owe it to my little old ladies and gentlemen to look like a host, a friend of theirs—which I am," he explained to Cherry "When you grow very, very old, a visit to the doctor may not be a cheerful occasion, unless we *make* it so."

Cherry said respectfully that she understood Dr. Lamb specialized in older people's ailments.

"Naturally I do! I have all the aches and pains myself, so I know where it hurts. Anyway, Miss Cherry, my patients have been with me a lifetime—and I'm too old now to take on any new ones. That's Grey's work. Well, young lady, Bill Fairall says you'll help me out whenever Mrs. Jackson can't."

Cherry said she would be glad to help. The old doctor glared at her. "I trust I can depend on you *not* to sneak into my office and 'clean it up' and 'straighten it out' and put everything in the wrong place!"

"Dr. Lamb, I will never touch anything in your office," Cherry promised with a straight face.

In the rush that morning Cherry had not seen Dottie Nash come in. But she was there, working in her lab, because her voice came over the intercom. Cherry saw the tall girl at noon, in her long white cotton coat, seated at one end of Mrs. Wick's desk. Dottie was telephoning for sandwiches and coffee to be sent in. No one had time to go out for lunch.

"What shall we order for you, Miss Ames—er—Cherry?" Dottie asked.

"Oh, anything. That's not very helpful, is it?" Cherry said. "Whatever you're having."

"Whatever we order, it won't be much good," Irene Wick complained. "And expensive. I'm going to bring lunch from my own kitchen one of these days! Dottie," Irene asked, "how was the party? Did you have a nice time?" Her tone to Dottie was gracious but patronizing.

The part-time R.N., Mrs. Rhoda Jackson, passed through the room, saying, "Mrs. Wick, Dr. Russell says we'll need more novocaine and more vitamin B12 shots when you reorder."

It was part of the medical secretary's job to purchase medications, medical instruments, office supplies, even new furniture if needed in the waiting room, and cleaning and laundry services. By keeping inventory of what was needed, then acting as purchasing agent, Irene Wick saved the three physicians considerable time to allocate to their patients.

Irene Wick made a note of the items the part-time nurse had requested. "Cherry, any reorders for you when I phone our supplier? I think we need more penicillin. Mrs. Jackson, how are your children?"

"Just fine, thanks." The part-time nurse sped off. She wasted no time on being friendly, either to the staff or to patients. She did a nursing job that was precise, reliable, and—well, mechanical. Cherry realized that Mrs. Jackson's main interest was in her young children, which was right, but she wished she could work up a little interest in others, too. Particularly in the sick, sometimes frightened, often suffering men and women who came to a doctor's office, seeking help; seeking a little sympathy and encouragement, too.

Dottie Nash said, "Mrs. Jackson giggles occasionally. I s'pose it's to prove she's human."

Mrs. Wick said gently, "Your remark isn't in the best of taste, I'm afraid," but she looked amused. "I suspect Rhoda Jackson resents having to work, even temporarily. However, she is entitled to her feelings—and to her privacy."

Cherry was startled by the substantial sums of money that flowed into the office. None of the three doctors' fees were unusually high. But Dr. Fairall had a large, lively practice, and the youngest and oldest doctors each had a sizable practice, too. Every day several hundred dollars came in, in the form of patients' checks in the mail, or checks and cash that patients handed to the nearest white-uniformed girl.

The first time a patient on leaving handed Cherry several folded bills, she didn't know what to do with the cash. Irene, who took care of all business details, was busy elsewhere at the moment. So Cherry wrote down the patient's name, the amount, and the date; then clipped the note to the money and put it in her uniform pocket. She turned it over ten minutes later to the medical secretary, who laughed at Cherry's question.

"But, Cherry, this *is* our system! Dottie, you, I, Mrs. Jackson—whichever of us is around—accepts payment.

Then—Come look at this file—" Irene Wick pulled open a file drawer to show Cherry. "Then you find the patient's card and write down how much was paid."

"And I put the cash into a cash drawer in your desk, or something like that?"

"No—you—don't! With so many people streaming in and out of here, the cash drawer was rifled several times. Our pockets are a safer place. At the end of the day," the medical secretary said, "I collect all cash from you and Dottie, and Rhoda Jackson if she's in. I figure from the cards what share goes to each doctor, and I take it to them. You know, our doctors don't have time to keep close track of income and outgo; they rely on me to keep the records straight," Irene Wick said with a certain pride.

"I take some or all of the cash to the bank—whatever each doctor doesn't want to keep in his pocket—along with checks and bankbooks, and make deposits in each doctor's account. Then I bring each doctor his bank receipt."

Cherry said doubtfully, "I'm sure the system works if you are satisfied with it, but—it—it sounds so hasty and informal. Just suppose one girl were even a little dishonest—would anyone ever notice, with all the emergencies and phone calls and pressure of work around here?"

"Quite right, Cherry. The doctors could easily be cheated. Of small sums, anyway—five dollars here, ten dollars there. About one-third of the patients pay cash in the office. But almost all doctors' offices use this system—I've worked in several. And in the two years I've worked here," said Mrs. Wick, "everyone has been—well, *devoted* to Dr. Fairall and Grey and dear old Lamb. They're wonderful men. They do terribly vital work. That's why I—perhaps—take more responsibility upon myself than my job requires."

Cherry asked what her duties were. The medical secretary enumerated them: make appointments, act as receptionist, send out bills, receive and record patients' payments, order and pay for supplies, and keep inventory of these, keep patients' case records typed up-to-date and accessible—handle the mail and the doctors' correspondence—and, biggest job of all, do the bookkeeping.

"I do an audit every three months," the medical secretary said. "Then I give the figures to our tax accountant, who estimates the doctors' quarterly tax payments. Besides, I think it's important to analyze regularly how things stand financially for our doctors. It's the best way, too, to keep expenses under control."

Irene Wick certainly knew what she was doing!

"And aren't you assisting Dr. Fairall with a book he's writing?" Cherry asked.

"Yes, he dictates to me. Sometimes I go to the medical library for him to look up and verify some fine point." Irene Wick stared full at Cherry and said, "He does rely quite specially on me."

"Good for you," said Cherry.

"I've been doing some of the nursing or assisting myself," Irene Wick told Cherry. "For a while we didn't have a nurse here, and I was pleasantly surprised at all I was able to do for our doctors."

Cherry was rather annoyed. The overtone said plainly: We don't need you here, Miss Nurse. Go away. Cherry asked as evenly as she could:

"What nursing did you do?"

"Oh, I weighed the patients, and once I gave a patient some Vitamin B, on Dr. Fairall's order. In another case I gave an injection. Dr. Lamb showed me how."

Cherry did not bother to say this was scarcely nursing. No point arguing. The best thing was to reassure Irene Wick that her job, her value and importance here, were *not* jeopardized by the presence of a graduate nurse.

So it was no wonder that Mrs. Wick seemed a little resentful and hurt when Dr. Fairall made a decision late that Thursday. From now on Cherry, the graduate nurse, not the medical secretary, was to be "first in command" in the office—in case of any emergencies, differences of opinion, or judgment. Irene Wick did not say anything, but she walked stiffly past Cherry, and stood drumming her fingers on her desk.

Cherry felt sorry. The woman apparently took pride in being of service here. Better to keep a tactful distance for a while. Cherry was actually glad when a medical supplier's salesman came in presently and asked for Mrs. Wick.

He had extraordinary milk-white skin and reddish hair. A small, gentle, young man, he seemed the very opposite of the usual aggressive salesman. He spoke to Cherry shyly, almost apologetically.

"My name is Bally, Alex Bally. Here's my card—" He asked Cherry her name and she told him. "Mrs. Wick knows me. In fact, Miss Ames, she does most of her business with my firm, so if you'd just tell her Bally is here—"

"Certainly," said Cherry, and rang the lab where Irene had gone.

When Irene Wick came in, she asked Cherry quite formally whether *she* wanted to order the medical supplies from Bally. Cherry said, "Of course not, Irene. Managing and administering and purchasing is *your* job. My job is nursing."

The medical secretary looked enormously relieved. Then she said very low to Cherry, "You're a dear."

Afterward, Cherry thought that her job here was *not only* nursing. Dr. Fairall had put her in charge, in a supervisory sense. So it was up to her to be continuously aware of everything going on in this busy office, and to maintain the morale of the staff.

~~~~~~

CHAPTER IV

A Young Ballet Dancer

FRIDAY MORNING AT DR. FAIRALL'S CHERRY HEARD SUCH a wild commotion—it sounded like splintering wood, thumps, yells, and a car backfiring—that she ran to the street windows in alarm. A dilapidated station wagon, sagging under a load of household articles, was parked in front of the brownstone. Standing on the sidewalk and solemnly surveying the station wagon were two young men. One was very tall, very thin, with long hair to his bony shoulders and a ferocious beard, dressed all in black. Cherry couldn't decide whether he was wearing a costume or gym clothes. The other young man, with wavy golden hair, was strikingly handsome. He wore swim trunks, an over-size sweatshirt, and was whistling "Dixie" off-key. He broke off to say:

"First let's take care of the baby's crib. Wouldn't want it to get smashed."

"Neither smashed, mashed, nor bashed," a basso voice issued from the lanky giant. "Nor boiled, oiled, nor spoiled."

Cherry was so fascinated that she opened the door to hear better, and stood just inside.

"My dear Will Shakespeare," exclaimed a woman's voice, "will you *please* not touch the crib! Henry J., won't you carry it up yourself?"

"Yes, Mrs. Faunce, don't worry," the handsome Henry J. called back. He opened the station wagon's rear door, reached in, and put a straw hat on his head against the hot sun.

"Mistrusted, disgusted, and busted," intoned the giant. He walked around the station wagon and bowed to the driver's seat. "Help you out, Mrs. Faunce?"

He handed out a tiny, perfectly beautiful old lady who appeared to be every inch a duchess. Cherry was working with Dr. Grey Russell that morning, but hoped he would not need her for another few minutes, because this performance was not to be missed. She stepped out of the doorway and said, experimentally, "Good morning."

"Oh, hi," said Henry J., and busily turned his back on her. Cherry noticed that his old sweatshirt carried in faint letters, nearly laundered out: *Texas*.

The silver-haired duchess smiled at Cherry and said, "Dr. Fairall has kindly offered Leslie and Henry J.—"

"I," the giant boomed at Cherry, "am the prophet Elijah." And he glanced down at her to see whether he had startled or otherwise impressed her. Cherry just grinned.

"—use of the vacant apartment on the top floor of his building," Her Grace explained to Cherry. "As you see, we are moving in. Not Elijah nor I—we're merely helping. Are you Dr. Fairall's nurse?"

Cherry introduced herself. Dr. Fairall must have made a quick decision to lend the Youngs the vacant apartment. Since he was treating an emergency at the hospital that morning, he had not yet had a chance to notify his office staff.

"Well, welcome," Cherry said. "I'm sorry we didn't know you were coming—so soon, I mean. We'd have had the apartment cleaned up a bit for you. Perhaps we still can, Mrs. Wick will know."

"We *had* to come pronto," Henry J. said, looking up at her from under the straw hat. He was bent nearly double under a rolled-up mattress that the bearded one was placing on his back. "Our rent is due at the other place, and we haven't got it. We're on the point of eviction. Whew! Is there an elevator, Miss Ames? Don't I remember one?"

"Yes. A tiny one. I'll show you—" Cherry led the way into the house. Henry J. and the duchess followed, and the giant carrying the baby's crib.

Irene Wick met them at the door. She looked terribly puzzled, mostly by the mattress.

Cherry said serenely, "Mrs. Wick, perhaps you already know Mrs. Faunce, the prophet Elijah, and Henry J.—is it Young?"

Irene Wick laughed. "So that's who it is under the hat! Of course I know Henry—and Leslie and the baby. And I should know you, Mrs. Faunce." She ushered in the little old lady. "I've heard so much about you—what a wonderful babysitter you are! I've often seen your late husband, in many roles. He was a great actor."

"Thank you, Mrs. Wick. I have heard so much of you, too. Yes, Adrian Faunce was a great actor."

The lady smoothed her worn dress. Cherry noticed that her shoes, too, were old. Evidently her husband had been improvident to leave his widow so poor. Or he may have had the actor's usual struggle, in spite of his talents, to earn a steady living. The Actors' Fund helped many aging performers and their families, but Mrs. Faunce looked too vigorous to retire willingly to an old actors' home.

Elijah—his name really was Nick, Cherry found out later, and he was currently playing the role of the prophet in a church play, hence his beard and long locks—had already tramped up the stairs with the crib. First Mrs. Wick and the old lady, then Henry J. and the mattress, rode upstairs in the elevator. Cherry went back to work. The young ballet dancer and her baby would arrive as soon as the apartment was in some kind of order.

At lunchtime Cherry went upstairs to see if she could help.

Cherry found the little old lady making peanut-butter sandwiches in quantity, as fast as she could.

In the living room a hi-fi record player poured forth the liquid, rolling accents of a Welsh poet declaiming his verses. Here the two young men were busy arranging on mantel and shelves a collection of programs announcing celebrated plays and ballets, in several countries and languages. In the bedroom the mattress was still rolled up. A mobile—a school of paper fish hung from a ribbon—floated over the baby's crib, which was flanked by green plants.

"Leslie says her plants cheer her up," Henry J. remarked as Cherry returned to the living room. She nearly stumbled over a big box of books and photographs, and a small box of dishes and groceries. "Have a sandwich, Miss Ames? A peanut butter or a pickle sandwich?"

"Thanks, no. Anything I can do to help?" Cherry asked. Henry J. said No.

The tall, thin, bearded young man glared at her. "You look disgustingly clean!" He waved his arms in sweeping protest. "Are you always so clean?"

"Ugh, yes, revolting," and Cherry went away, giggling.

About half past four she heard the now familiar spatter of backfiring—then a baby crying and a girl's soft voice in the front hall. Cherry was helping Dr. Fairall.

Irene Wick stopped by to whisper that the two boys had brought Leslie in a wheelchair and that she looked quite weak. As soon as Dr. Fairall conscientiously could leave his gallbladder patient, he went upstairs. After an interval he came back and asked Mrs. Wick to order from the corner drugstore some iron and liver medication for Leslie, to build her up.

"Have they the money to pay for iron and liver vitamins?" Mrs. Wick asked. "That's expensive."

"Probably not," Dr. Fairall said. "Put it on my charge account, if necessary."

"Oh, Doctor, you shouldn't!" the medical secretary exclaimed. "Haven't we something else on hand that would do?"

"You know, Irene," Bill Fairall said impatiently, "there are more important considerations than money."

In the silence Cherry felt uncomfortable at having to witness this rebuke. Then the medical secretary said:

"Excuse me, Doctor. It's just that you already treat so many people without charge." Mrs. Wick smiled at him flatteringly. Dr. Fairall did not look up from writing at his desk.

Presently Dr. Fairall said, "Cherry—and you, Irene—go upstairs whenever you get a chance, will you? Those kids need help. Sorry if I was abrupt, Irene. You know what a wild day I'm having."

Cherry would have asked permission to go up for a visit anyway. It was nice being urged to go.

She went upstairs after her day's work was finished. She found the apartment halfway livable now—"livable for a gypsy," Cherry thought, stepping over empty soda bottles. Henry J. ushered Cherry in and cordially invited her to stay for dinner.

"We're having chopped beef forestière, with mushrooms, parsley, and a dash of—er—something. I'm preparing it from a cookbook. Or if you'd rather, Miss Ames, you can share the baby's cereal."

A girl's matter-of-fact voice called tiredly from the bedroom, "We are having plain hamburgers, with a dish of cereal, dear Henry. This isn't the day for gourmet cooking."

Cherry rapped on the open bedroom door. "May I come in? I'm Dr. Fairall's nurse." She was curious to meet the young ballerina, and, while not expecting some exquisite girl in drifts of tulle skirts and ribbontied slippers, Cherry was surprised at Leslie Young's appearance.

She was not a pretty girl; in fact, her features were odd and irregular. Her straight, dark hair was slicked back and tied into two pigtails. Yet the total effect was arresting, memorable. Leslie was on the tall side, thin to the point of boniness, and obviously weak as she lay on the bed in blue jeans and cotton shirt. Even so, she had a lanky grace, poise, an odd distinctiveness.

"She's an original," Cherry thought. "She'd stand out anywhere."

"I'm glad to meet you, Cherry Ames," said the young dancer. "Excuse me for not getting up, but I can't. Isn't it stupid?"

Cherry looked down into the girl's enormous, lackluster eyes. "When did you last have something to eat, Leslie? And I wish you'd call me Cherry."

"Hi, Cherry. This morning. An egg."

"I'm great at broiling hamburgers," said Henry J., standing in the doorway. "I did cook the cereal."

"Then will you please feed the baby when he wakes up," Leslie said. "And I wish so much, darling, that you wouldn't talk baby talk to him."

"Why not? He's a baby," said Henry J.

"He's a person. He's *somebody*," said Leslie, "so let's not insult him with inanities."

"May I meet your son?" Cherry asked

Henry J. proudly led her to the crib where a husky, rosy baby lay blinking and yawning, wiggling his tiny fingers and toes.

"He's trying to wake up," Henry J. murmured.

"What a fine, big boy!" Cherry exclaimed.

Leslie said, "Thank you. He's named after his daddy," and she beamed.

"*Glub!*" said the baby cheerfully. "*Flambp!*"

"Yes, indeed," Leslie answered. "That's right," Henry J. encouraged him. Another voice said, "Glub to you, too, young fellow. May I come in?"

It was Grey Russell. He wanted to meet "our new neighbors." The Youngs were interested to meet Dr. Fairall's quiet young relief doctor. They all talked for a few minutes, about the one thing they had in common—knowing Bill Fairall. Leslie said, "He's been wonderful to us."

"Imagine letting us use this apartment," Henry J. said. "I hate to accept it rent free. A man at Elijah's garage got me a job driving a taxi from midnight until eight. Relieving some of the regular drivers. I start tonight."

"We-ll," Leslie said, "I hope you can stay awake. It's really not a practical plan for an actor."

Grey Russell, who was just a little older than Henry J., listened thoughtfully.

"It isn't practical?" Henry J. said vaguely. "No, I suppose not. The taxi job will interfere with my making the rounds of the casting offices."

Cherry said it was high time Leslie had some food—time for her and Dr. Russell to leave.

Grey Russell was on his way to the dentist. He drove Cherry home. He was sorry he hadn't time to accept her invitation to come in for potluck supper with the Spencer Club.

"I'd like to meet your friends," he said. "I'd like it just to get acquainted with you. No real chance during working hours, is there? Will you have supper with me Sunday evening?"

"Why, thanks," Cherry said, trying not to sound surprised. "I'd love to."

"Tell you what. I'll call for you at seven, and we'll go to the Stage Door. We'll dine in the garden." Cherry looked so puzzled that the young doctor laughed. "That's a new restaurant here in the Village, run by a bunch of kids who are in, or want to be in, the theater. Sounds like fun. Let's try it."

Grey let her off at her door, No. 9 Standish Street.

"You've made a date with Dr. Russell for Sunday evening?" Gwen, Bertha, and Josie were pleased for her, but puzzled when Cherry told them. "That's nice," Bertha said. "But have you forgotten that this weekend we're driving out to Long Island, to look at the house? And do some preliminary work there?"

Cherry said of course she was going with them and would work as hard as anyone. "I'll just take the train back to the city late Sunday afternoon."

Early the next morning the four girls started out with high hopes, sunglasses and sun hats, and necessary cleaning equipment.

In Gwen's car they left Manhattan Island via the Queens Midtown Tunnel for Long Island, and rode along green parkways. The traffic was light that early, and they went skimming along in the morning sun. Big apartment buildings beyond the parkway were left behind. They passed fewer houses, smaller towns, churches, airports. The girls began to smell a salty breeze. After a while they began watching for their exit from the parkway.

It took them onto a quiet country highway, past meadows and barns, then right into the lovely elm-shaded village of Prescott.

"Look, there's the library—and the old meeting hall!" Gwen pointed out, driving slowly. "And the church, they've repainted the steeple—"

The village dated back to pre-Revolutionary Days. Cherry recognized it as a bit of New England. The public buildings faced a grassy commons, with its statue of Nathan Hale. The wooden buildings and houses, simple and classic in design, were painted a sparkling white. Low white picket fences enclosed lawns and the widely separated houses. Over all towered the centuries-old elm trees.

"So serene, so dignified," Bertha breathed.

"Where is everyone?" Josie asked. "All I see are dogs and birds and those two little boys on bicycles."

"Look ahead," Cherry said. People and parked cars clustered around a grocery store with a gasoline pump out in front, a small post office, a shop displaying sports clothes, a barbershop, a hardware store, and a small restaurant. "Why, this is a metropolis!"

"Well, for a mostly summer place, yes," Gwen answered.

They drove half a mile along the main street. Gwen turned off down a dirt lane. "Our estate!" she announced, and stopped the car.

At first the girls could see only flowering bushes and trees, and beyond, a long stretch of meadow. A huge old red barn stood far away at its end. Gwen led the way. Just on the other side of the shielding bushes and trees stood a rambling, one-story weather-stained house. With its porch around all four sides, and flower beds blooming wild, the place looked inviting—and dilapidated.

"It *is* a mess." Gwen's face puckered as if she might cry.

"We'll make it shipshape again," Bertha said confidently.

A bird sang somewhere over their heads. The girls stood listening. A scent of roses and the hum of bees came to them on waves of soft air.

"It's lovely here!" Cherry exclaimed. She felt so happy to be outdoors that she would willingly camp out in a pup tent, if necessary. "Come on. Let's explore!"

Gwen had the house key ready in her hand. First, though, they walked around the porch, littered with last autumn's leaves. They found rocking chairs, weather-beaten but still serviceable. "The leaves are dry, we'll make a bonfire," Bertha said. She started back to the car for a broom. But the other girls said, "Oh, let's do our grand survey first."

Several fine shade trees stood in the deep, over-grown grass. Gwen looked for and found the brick bar-becue grill. "It's in pretty good condition," she called. "We'll have cookouts!" An old well, when the girls leaned over cautiously and looked into it, sent up a cold draft, dim reflections of their faces—it was full of rainwater and spooky echoes.

"If this place has any ghosts," Josie said, "he or she or *it* probably lives in the well."

"How do you know?" Cherry challenged.

"It's where I'd choose to stay, if I were a ghost," Josie offered. She couldn't quite keep her face straight.

Cherry, sniffing, located the fragrant wild roses. They all admired a row of hydrangea bushes that in summer would be loaded with giant balls of blue flowers.

"When do we go to the beach?"

"We haven't toured the house yet!"

"Or the barn!"

The red barn appeared to be an eighth mile away from the house—about two or three city blocks. Bertha said the barn would be a project in itself, and she knew, having grown up on a farm. "Let's save the barn for later."

The four girls went into the house, which was dark, dusty, and still. They pulled up shades, opened windows wide—only two windows were badly stuck—and let in the sun and air. "An overgrown cottage, that's what this is!" Cherry said. One immense room served as both living room and dining room. Branching off it were three bedrooms, two small baths, and a kitchen.

Gwen dropped into a plump old leather chair. "My favorite chair!" she said, bouncing.

The furnishings in the main room were sketchy, but enough—a long oak dining table with benches, a wicker sofa with cushions, a few old easy chairs, tables, and lamps. Everything was battered, but useable with a fresh coat of paint or "just ten gallons of elbow grease," Josie said.

Bertha was going from bedroom to bedroom, poking and punching mattresses. She returned looking satisfied. "Comfortable. Twin beds in each room, a little dusty is all."

Six beds! Gwen said there used to be—yes, there still were—a couple of folding cots in the coat closet. They could sleep eight! They wished the other members of the Spencer Club could be here to enjoy this place, once it was made ready. It was a good vacation spot—a shame to let it stand unused between weekends, all summer!

Cherry could not help thinking of some of Dr. Fairall's less fortunate patients, who would appreciate a chance to rest and play in the country. Then Cherry thought of the exhausted young ballerina. Leslie urgently needed building up. Country air would do wonders for her, and for the baby. If Mrs. Faunce could come along to help look after them, it might be a sort of holiday for the little old lady, too.

It occurred to Cherry that—busy last evening with preparations to come out here—she had forgotten to tell the other three nurses about Leslie, Henry J., and little H.J. Young.

So Cherry told her friends now, as they took time out to enjoy the sandwiches and oranges Bertha had packed. Cherry hesitated to suggest or request inviting the Youngs, since this was Gwen's house—or, at least, the Spencer Club's house. To Cherry's great pleasure, Gwen responded at once. So did Bertha and Josie.

"Why, of course! Your ballerina could come out here for a week or two," Gwen offered. "We'll be here only weekends. Plenty of room! For her and the baby, and if Henry J. can come out to visit on his days off, fine."

Cherry said carefully, "Are you sure you want a six-month-old baby and a semi-invalid around?"

The other three stared at her, as if Cherry had forgotten they were nurses, used to getting along easily with invalids and babies, among others.

Gwen said to Cherry, "You'll have to find out whether she'd *want* to come—how her husband feels about it— What Dr. Fairall advises—"

"You know," Josie said, brushing a fleck of sandwich off her glasses, "if they *do* come, we'll have to hurry up and get this house ready, quick, quick. That's not so awful. I mean, it's an incentive for us." Since Josie was something of a dawdler and dreamer, this was a heroic speech.

"Quick, quick," Gwen echoed. "Well, let's see what needs to be done." She got out paper and pencil. She wrote three headings: *Urgent, Necessary,* and *Would Be Nice.* "Maybe we can do our survey and chores as we go along," Gwen said hopefully.

At the end of the day the four tired, grimy young nurses sat down on the porch steps (swept clean), to consider Gwen's pages and pages of notes. The *Urgent* list was the longest, and had the hardest things to do, such as: repair the house roof, clean out the barn. The *Necessary* list, too, called for hard work: mow the grass; air and sun the mattresses outdoors. *Would Be Nice* included: repair the barbecue grill, paint the furniture. "Grim," said Gwen.

The four girls sat there appalled, yawning, brooding.

"Well, we can invite our friends to help us transform this place," Gwen said. "We'll invite 'em for swims and picnics. Only every guest will have to do some chore. That'll be understood in advance. No work—no eat, no fun."

The other three muttered at her. "Optimist! Guests want to swim and gobble refreshments and go home. What makes you think they'll work?"

Gwen tenderly touched her sunburned nose. "Want to bet? Naturally some people won't accept. We'll invite everyone we know, acquaintances, friends of friends."

Bertha said soberly, "I think Gwen is right. Some people will help us. They do, back home in Minnesota. Only they'll do more things wrong than right." Cherry refused to be discouraged, and said so. Then she made a suggestion. "Let's drive to the beach, to cheer ourselves up. Then let's have dinner somewhere nice, and drive home—to the city—and go to bed."

That's what they did, knowing that if they stayed overnight here, or at a motel, and worked again tomorrow, they could not be fresh and alert on Monday morning for their next week's nursing work. And responsibility to their patients came first.

CHAPTER V

A Date at the Stage Door

"Your eyes are like melting gumdrops,
Your teeth are like grains of rice,
You're pigeon-toed and cross-eyed,
And I think you're horribly nice."

SO SANG THE YOUNG MAN STANDING IN FRONT OF Cherry and Grey's table, serenading them with a banjo. They and the other diners winced but applauded. The troubador hitched up his pants and strolled to the next table. Striking a chord, he started to declaim, "Friends, Romans, countrymen, lend me your ears—It was brillig in the slithey tove—"

"This Stage Door is the craziest restaurant I've ever been to," Cherry said to Grey, laughing. "Crazy even for Greenwich Village."

The walls were whitewashed brick, the tables and chairs were painted variously, red, blue, and yellow.

56

Paintings by local artists hung on one wall. Another wall was covered with photographs of actors. A mammoth jukebox was stocked with folk song, jazz, and foreign records. The young waiters and waitresses were dressed as famous characters from well-known plays. Old-time movies were shown at nine and midnight.

"It certainly is a Village-y place," Grey smiled back at Cherry. "The food is pretty good, though."

They had enjoyed bowls of chilled soup, then foot-long hot dogs—"enough to kill us," Grey said. Now they were working on a huge, spectacular sundae, called the Kitchen Sink, shared between them. They knew better than to assault their stomachs like this and both took pleasure in breaking all the sensible rules, for once.

A fat, foreign man at the next table had been listening to the banjo singer, and now cried out, "Very goo'! Very ni'! *Non che mala!*" The visitor burst into song himself, an operatic aria, rising to his feet and gesturing grandly.

He had a fine baritone, and was very much the opera star. So much so that the young singing waiters and waitresses who worked there "between theater jobs" looked jealous. A passing young waitress sniffed and muttered, "A vulture for culture." Everybody listened, then applauded the fat man. He bowed, perspiring, and sat down.

"That's all the crazy stuff I can stand for one evening," Grey said. "It will do me for several weeks. Shall we go?"

A sing-along session, with banjo and washboard accompaniment, was starting as Grey and Cherry left the restaurant.

The street was dark and quiet. They walked along twisting, picturesque alleys, to the tree-shadowed paths of Washington Square Park. Here on a summer's night men sat playing chess by moonlight, and couples looked deep into each other's eyes and ate ice cream on a stick. Families brought their children to hear college students in blue jeans sing folk songs and play guitars around the fountain.

"Pleasant here," Grey said. "Care to sit down?"

They searched for two seats together on the well-populated benches, found them, and settled down near the shadow-dappled buildings of New York University. The young doctor asked Cherry how she liked working in Dr. Fairall's office—for three doctors.

"Well, there's a good part and a not so bad part, a different part—" Cherry explained that she missed the intensive bedside care she had given in hospital wards and private duty cases. "I'm accustomed to nursing my patients every day—watching them gradually get well. But in the office I usually see a patient just a few times."

Some did come back often for a course of treatments. Most patients came only occasionally for an annual checkup, or to have the doctor examine them if they were not feeling well. Then they went home, and the nurse would not see them again for a while. Cherry knew she would read their medical follow-up, for the doctors wrote notes on these developments in the patients' case histories. She would talk to the patients on the phone, answer their questions about such things as diet and prescribed treatment.

She did value a nursing role in which she assisted with the thorough examination of patients. To this end, Cherry as office nurse was prepared to do some laboratory work—blood count, urinalysis, G.L. series (gastrointestinal)—if Dr. Fairall had not employed a laboratory technician. When the doctor performed minor surgery in the office, Cherry would sterilize the instruments, and work alongside the doctor as surgical nurse. She was entrusted with giving patients certain treatments, oral medication, injections, following the doctor's orders. Besides, Cherry had a special responsibility and this was "the best part"—patient contact, which meant giving emotional support and teaching good health habits.

"I love meeting dozens of people every day," she said to Grey. "Such variety! Some days my job is more psychology than medicine."

"Yes, that's true. As a doctor, I'm fascinated by the *medical* variety in private practice," Grey Russell said.

"Aren't you fascinated by seeing people from all walks of life?" Cherry asked. "And some of Dr. Fairall's theatrical people—! Have you ever treated Al Jenkins? I swear he's made of rubber. You should have seen him clowning in the treatment room. He talked doubletalk to me for a good five minutes before I caught on."

"Oh, yes, good old Alfalfa Jenkins," Grey said, and grinned. "He was in and out of the hospital with his faulty heart when I was a resident physician there. Well! Here we sit on a Sunday evening talking shop. Shall we walk a little more? What are you giggling about?"

"I just happened to think of old Dr. Lamb and the way he goes stamping around, roaring, 'Where's my what-chamacallit? Nurse! Who's been cleaning my *private* office and mislaid my whatchamacallit?'" Cherry laughed.

"He's a fine doctor, though," Grey said, laughing. "Come on. Let's walk off that Kitchen Sink sundae." They strolled back across the park, then past the great, sculptured Washington Arch.

Grey and Cherry emerged onto lower Fifth Avenue with its skyscraper apartment buildings and elegant hotels. People dined at an attractive sidewalk cafe, sheltered by hedges and awnings; uniformed captains and waiters bustled to serve them.

"Slightly different from where we were," Grey said with a chuckle.

Cherry looked at the diners, then stared. "Grey! See that table where the captain is just bringing that flaming dessert?—or whatever it is. See the woman there?"

"Yes, I see a woman and a man. Incidentally, she's middle-aged—but he's only about thirty."

"Isn't she our medical secretary, Mrs. Irene Wick?" The reddish-haired, milky-skinned man with Mrs. Wick—now who was he? Cherry was sure she had seen him in the doctor's office.

Grey and Cherry slowed their stroll to a stop. He pretended to search for something in his jacket pocket, murmuring, "Yes, it is Irene Wick. Beautiful outfit she's wearing. Who's that with her?"

Cherry was busy noticing Mrs. Wick's expensive flower-laden hat, and the numerous silver platters that a waiter had just removed from their table. What an elaborate dinner. But why? Surely not a romance? The cold, bored look on Mrs. Wick's face was not romantic.

Then she recognized the man. He was Bally, the salesman. The one from whom Mrs. Wick bought most of the three doctors' medications and supplies. Playing favorites? But Mrs. Wick had said Bally's prices were lower, for the same items and quality, than the prices of the salesmen from other supply houses. Mrs. Wick had distinctly said she saved money for her employers by buying chiefly from Bally.

Just the same, Cherry thought, it looked odd for Irene to be accepting such an expensive dinner from Bally. As if Bally were rewarding her for throwing her employer's purchases his way. Cherry said as much to Grey Russell, as they walked on.

"I agree with you," he said, "except that 'business entertaining' is commonplace. Bally earns a commission on every sale he makes. Our medical secretary, who buys supplies for *three* physicians and our laboratory, is a valuable customer. If Bally wants to provide Irene with an incentive to buy from him instead of from his competitors—well, it's legal."

"I can't help feeling she's trading on her position in Dr. Fairall's office," Cherry said.

"Sure she is," Grey said. "Still, it's just a dinner. Call it Bally's expression of thanks, or good will."

"It isn't strictly ethical of her to accept," Cherry insisted.

"Right. It's a small matter, though. I imagine Bill Fairall wouldn't mind." Grey sounded bored. He said in a livelier tone, "I had an idea during dinner about Henry J."

Cherry was glad to change the subject to something more pleasant.

"Instead of driving a taxi all night," the young doctor said, "why couldn't Henry J. be one of the waiter-entertainers at the Stage Door? If he'd want to, that is. He'd have better hours and be able to give Leslie and the baby more help. He'd probably earn more, too."

"And have more fun at his work," Cherry said.

"I know some of the people who operate the restaurant," Grey said. "They're always looking for talented young people. No sooner do they train a boy or a girl to wait on tables, than he or she leaves for a job in a play or with a touring company."

"We'll ask Henry J.," Cherry said. "What do you suppose the J. stands for?"

Grey laughed. "Some awful name, probably. I'll bet we never find out."

CHAPTER VI

Strange Happenings

~~~~~~

MRS. WICK GREETED CHERRY AT THE BROWNSTONE AT seven-thirty the next morning with a friendly smile, and no mention of having seen each other last evening on Fifth Avenue. She still had her hat on—her everyday hat—as she turned on lights and air conditioning, and put the sterilizers on.

"Thanks," Cherry said, busy getting out medical supplies. She wasn't going to mention last evening, either. "We have a patient coming in early for an injection before she goes to work—it's Miss Hardy." The nurse gave injections on the doctor's order, usually vitamins or liver or influenza vaccine. "And Mr. Gatti, the infected finger case, is coming in at eight for a blood test," Cherry said.

The telephones started ringing. Cherry and the medical secretary grabbed them. Cherry had to cope tactfully with an old lady who had had a summer cold for a month now, but "must see Dr. Lamb the minute he comes in." The next phone call was from a long-winded young man who probably would take up more of Dr. Fairall's time than most patients. Cherry scheduled him in the appointment book accordingly. An office nurse had to be a psychologist—had to size up people.

When one man telephoned that he had nausea and pain in the abdomen, Cherry could hear from his breathing that he was not exaggerating. Cherry wrote down his name, address, telephone number, and symptoms. She cautioned him to take no foods, no water, no laxatives. "If you have an icebag—that will relieve your pain. Dr. Russell will call you back shortly." The symptoms indicated appendicitis.

She gave the message to Irene, who was pulling the charts for patients coming in that day. Then Cherry ran upstairs to change into her uniform.

As she pinned on her nurse's cap, Cherry thought of the young family on the top floor. How were they this morning? She would try to go up to see them some time today and help out a little, and extend Gwen's offer.

The early patients began coming in. Cherry and Irene Wick took turns in greeting them—"I see you're right on time! We'll call you in just a few minutes. There are some new magazines on the table. . . ." Cherry did the bloodwork since the lab technician had not arrived yet, gave the injection, wrote a memo to Dottie Nash asking for the findings on the Gatti hemoglobin (iron) count. Where was the lab technician? Dottie was late this morning. Cherry thought perhaps she had better do the Gatti blood count herself. She heard Mrs. Wick on the phone ordering so many c.c.'s of various drugs, smallpox vaccine, B12, adrenalin, typhoid shots, tetanus vaccine, novocaine, and penicillin. At the end, the medical secretary said, "You're welcome, Mr. Bally."

Dottie Nash hurried in, mumbling apologies for being late. Mrs. Wick asked her, "Did you have a good time at the dance?"

"Oh, I had a marvelous time! I did buy that dress— remember the one I told you about, Mrs. Wick—the blue? It took some managing. I'll tell you about it later." Dottie Nash giggled, a silly, tiny sound to issue from such a big girl. "Oh, hello, Miss Ames," she said, and clattered off to her laboratory.

Cherry gave the lab technician a few minutes to get her work set up. Meanwhile, she checked with the roentgenologist to whom the doctors sent patients for X-ray therapy. Dr. Fairall was having one man's lesions treated by X ray.

Then Cherry started for the lab carrying Mr. Gatti's blood sample. Down the long hall, she heard Mrs. Wick's voice. Cherry could not make out the words. But the rage—not annoyance, but rage—made Cherry wonder. What had caused Irene to change so suddenly toward Dottie? It must be something serious to arouse such fury. Had Dottie made some mistake in her work? If a medical mistake was involved here, she'd better find out, Cherry decided.

Irene Wick burst out of the lab, rigid and pale. She stamped along the hall into an empty examining room and slammed the door shut.

Cherry waited, then rapped at the open lab door. Receiving no reply, she went in. Dottie Nash, perched on a high lab stool, was crying like a clumsy, overgrown child.

"Why, Dottie, things can't be that bad," Cherry said humorously.

"Oh, can't they! I'm going to be in trouble—all because of that Mrs. Wick. I thought she was my friend! I haven't done anything bad, honestly, Miss Ames. Just a little indiscreet—foolish—"

"Has it anything to do with your work here?" Cherry asked. "Perhaps I can help you straighten it out. You know, Dottie, everyone makes mistakes."

Dottie looked down at her hands, then out the lab window. "Thanks, Miss Ames, but it has nothing to do with my work." She sniffled and gulped. "I don't make mistakes in the lab. Only outside. You can check my work if you want. This is a personal thing. Between Mrs. Wick and me."

"Would you like me to put in a good word for you with Mrs. Wick?"

"No." Dottie stood up, blew her nose, and said shakily, "Want me to analyze that blood sample?"

"Yes, please, as soon as you have time," Cherry said. "I'm sorry you are so upset. You don't really believe Mrs. Wick would do anything to injure you?"

"No, I suppose not." Dottie Nash wiped her eyes. "You can't tell about Irene Wick, though. She drove Zelda away—Zelda Colt. She was so nasty and uncooperative that Zelda just couldn't stand working here any more!"

Cherry silently discounted Dottie's overexcited statement. She asked who Zelda Colt was.

"The full-time registered nurse who was here before you," the technician said.

"Did she resign?" Cherry asked.

"No, Dr. Fairall fired her. Zelda left here under a cloud. Sort of mysterious. I never found out exactly."

Cherry was startled. She doubted that any R.N. would permit a medical secretary to drive her off a job. Besides, Mrs. Wick, though touchy and bossy, did not seem to be malicious. Yet—why had Nurse Colt been dismissed?

Cherry would not stoop to gossiping with the staff. She asked Grey Russell, but the young doctor said, "Office politics. I don't know the details." She would not bother elderly Dr. Lamb with questions.

The next day Cherry found an opportune moment to ask Dr. Fairall privately how her work compared with her predecessor's.

"If I can improve my performance, Doctor, or if I'm omitting to do something Miss Colt did—?"

"You're a better nurse than Colt!" His rather heavy, handsome face tightened. "I'd just as soon not discuss Colt. A painful subject. Nothing *you* can learn from it, Cherry."

The other nurse certainly had left under a cloud! Dr. Fairall saw Cherry's embarrassment and said:

"All right, I'll tell you. In confidence. You'd better know, in case some of our patients prove difficult to get along with. Maybe it's because Colt was unkind to them."

"Unkind! A nurse?" Cherry exclaimed.

Bill Fairall impatiently rose from his desk and paced the room. "Oh, don't talk like an idiot! Do you think every nurse, every doctor, is perfection?" He was so angry—with what Zelda Colt had done to his patients—that he glared and sputtered.

"You know what, Cherry? With a disabled patient, Colt refused to tie his shoes when he couldn't get down to 'em. Refused other times to help Lamb's very old ladies zip or unzip a dress. Brusque. Unkind. Snapped at a sick person. Made a person feel he is a nuisance—no right to be here."

Cherry murmured, "That's hard to believe. I suppose some patients complained to you?"

Dr. Fairall stopped pacing and ran his hands over his face. "Actually no patient complained to me. I don't encourage whining, you know, or self-pity! No, Colt's poor behavior was brought to my attention by—by another source."

By Mrs. Wick? Cherry wondered. Were the charges true?

"Dr. Fairall, had Nurse Colt actually done these things?"

"Of course she did!" Then, he stopped and amended that. "I have every reason to believe she did, Cherry, because I can trust my informant. But I myself never saw Colt behave badly to a patient. Naturally, she wouldn't in front of me—her employer!"

"And you couldn't very well go to the patients and ask," Cherry said. "That would be unprofessional, wouldn't it?"

Dr. Fairall snorted. "A doctor is supposed to *know* what his staff is doing. He can't go ask a question like that, anyway." He hesitated, then rushed on, "And if it was true, a hypersensitive patient might get upset by my question."

"I see," said Cherry. She did see, but she recalled Dottie's statement that Mrs. Wick had driven the nurse away.

Why? Why had Irene Wick wanted Nurse Colt out of here? Could it be because Zelda Colt had ignored—or even trampled on—Mrs. Wick's great desire to be important around here, to take charge, to be greatly needed and valuable?

"Dr. Fairall, it you don't mind my asking," Cherry said, "what was Miss Colt like? Was she really harsh?"

"I never found her so. She may have appeared harsh to others. A little tactless, too outspoken. A little humorless. Very conscientious and reliable, one of those brisk, hard-working, efficient, middle-aged women—hard-driving—like Irene Wick."

The comparison startled Cherry. Had the nurse and the medical secretary been competitors to be Number One in running the office?

Dr. Fairall's telephone rang. A friend was inviting him to play tennis late that afternoon. He smiled and said, "I'll be there, Ed, and I'll beat you this time."

The doctor hung up. He said to Mrs. Wick, who was just coming in, bringing her stenographer's notebook, "Please call my wife. Tell her I'll be home half an hour later than we planned. Where are we going this evening?"

"I bought tickets for you and your guests to the visiting ballet company from London," she replied.

So she was a social secretary sometimes, too, Cherry thought. Mrs. Wick was very close to Dr. Fairall, both in his professional and private life. Well, it was part of her job to know his whereabouts at all times.

"Fine! Thanks, Irene. And thank you, Cherry," Dr. Fairall said, to let her know she could go now. Irene's notebook meant Dr. Fairall was now going to dictate either letters or more of his book. "Speaking of ballet," he said, "have either of you had a chance to visit Leslie?"

Irene Wick smiled deferentially at him. "I run upstairs frequently. I heard about Cherry bathing the baby on Monday."

"I heard about your preparing their lunch on Monday and Tuesday," Cherry replied. The doctor beamed impartially.

"It's nothing. I love to cook," Mrs. Wick said. "I ought to do lunch for you, Dr. Fairall."

Cherry felt puzzled. Irene Wick was contradictory. Having prepared lunch for the Youngs upstairs, Mrs. Wick almost *had* to offer to prepare lunch for Dr. Fairall. Yet she was doing far more acts of kindness for the Youngs than Dr. Fairall had requested.

But how did such generosity and conscientiousness compare with her accepting that lavish dinner from the salesman, Bally?

What about Dottie Nash's describing the gracious Mrs. Wick as "nasty and uncooperative" with the other nurse?

What about Mrs. Wick's repeated urging of Cherry not to come to work so early, nor to stay so late? Was there something going on that she would rather Cherry did not observe?

Why had Dottie been so bitterly afraid of Mrs. Wick the other day?

Their relations had improved by now. On Thursday Cherry went into the lab to get some information. She found Mrs. Wick there with Dottie, like a sleek, poised mother cat with a clumsy, eager kitten.

Dottie seemed happy to be back in Mrs. Wick's good graces. She tried awkwardly with Cherry to take back what she had revealed about the medical secretary— what she had blurted out in anger and fright. Why fright?

Another thing Cherry did not understand occurred toward the end of that second week in June. A young salesman named Ted Bernstein complained to Cherry, half-humorously, that "I can't even sell Mrs. Wick a single, solitary, blessed item! My prices are attractive—no one undersells my firm. We have a wonderful, complete line of supplies, first-rate in everything. Now, why won't your Mrs. Wick give me even a little, tiny order?"

And an older, quiet salesman for still another medical supply house, a gray-haired man named Joseph La Cava, said to Cherry, "Mrs. Wick won't let me talk to any of the doctors—too busy doctoring to see a salesman, I understand. So may I talk to you, Miss Ames? I'd like to know whether there's any point in my calling at this office any longer. In a year Mrs. Wick hasn't yet placed an order with my firm. It doesn't seem fair that Mr. Bally has a monopoly, does it? Ah—excuse me, Miss Ames—but does Dr. Fairall know about this monopoly?"

Cherry brought Mrs. Wick's purchasing practices to Dr. Fairall's attention, privately, impersonally. He was busy as usual—rushing between hospital and operating room and a colleague's office.

"I'll take it up with Irene," Dr. Fairall said absently. He made a note to himself to do so.

Dr. Fairall never said another word to Cherry on this subject. He was too preoccupied by his work and many other interests to pay much attention to the management of the office. It did run smoothly, with never an annoyance or intrusion for the three doctors, Cherry acknowledged.

She still thought the cash-into-uniform-pocket a sloppy method of accepting patients' payments. Some days she carried around a hundred dollars in her uniform pocket; there must be much more cash in Mrs. Wick's pocket. Yet when she checked with her Spencer Club nurse friends they said that was the way it was done in every doctor's office they knew of. At Dr. Fairall's they *could* have a little safe, but were much too busy to fuss with it. Cherry noticed that each staff person in her office carefully marked each patient's charge card Paid. However, it still seemed to her this system of handling the doctors' money was awfully casual.

Cherry found it was useless to suggest any change in methods to Irene Wick. Irene was set in her ways. On Friday morning Cherry suggested that Dr. Fairall might dictate his book into a tape recorder rather than squander Irene's time by having her take it down in shorthand. Irene nearly bit Cherry's head off.

"I'm sorry," Cherry said. "I only meant that you already work so hard—"

"Didn't you know," said Mrs. Wick, "that the doctor discusses his book with me, as we go along? He can't do that with a machine!"

Perfectly true. Cherry was appalled at how tactless she had been. To make up for it, she offered during a lull late that afternoon to help Irene with the bookkeeping.

Irene was snowed under with a big pile of charge cards, showing doctors' charges and patients' payments. These figures had to be transferred, sooner or later, to the ledger—a tedious job. The account books also were needed, Cherry knew, to estimate the doctors' income taxes and so were open to government inspection for honesty.

"I could do a simple copying job," Cherry offered. "I'm careful, and if you like, I can—"

"I never let anyone touch these books but myself!" Irene Wick snapped at her. She was so tense that she quivered. Cherry stared, shocked. "Oh, I'm sorry," Mrs. Wick said. "By the end of Friday afternoon I'm dreadfully tired. Thanks, anyway, Cherry. The job's not as simple as it looks. I'd have to teach you. And one tiny error can take hours of rechecking."

They were interrupted by Cherry's having to talk on the phone to the R.N. in a specialist's office, where one of Dr. Fairall's patients had been referred. Cherry carefully wrote down the specialist's findings. Then, getting out the patient's chart, she asked the other R.N. a few medical questions that she felt Dr. Fairall would need to know.

Irene Wick touched her hand. "Finished phoning? I could use your help, if you'll forgive my stupid outburst." She seemed concerned that she might have offended Cherry, eager to erase a bad impression.

But Cherry had been stunned by Irene's jealousy about handling the books herself. This was the nearest she and the medical secretary had come to a quarrel.... Had Nurse Colt blundered into this domain of money? And so provoked Irene into being "nasty and uncooperative"? An idea struck Cherry. Had the other nurse found out something about Irene—something detrimental—a not too scrupulous honesty?

"You're so very quiet, Cherry," Mrs. Wick said gently. "I hope I haven't hurt your feelings."

"No, no. Not at all. Just tired—on Friday afternoons, end of the workweek, as you said," Cherry answered.

"Look, my dear," Irene Wick said. "If you *want* to work on the charge cards, or if you *want* to total what we took in in cash and checks today—certainly, go ahead."

"Irene Wick remembers that Dr. Fairall put me in charge here," Cherry thought. She felt terribly uncomfortable. She had a responsibility to her employer. On the other hand, she had to be entirely fair in supervising this woman who worked hard for her living.

"Come on, Cherry," Irene Wick urged her. "I'll show you how to read these ledgers, if you wish. Because

I don't want you to doubt even for a minute that I keep the records in anything but perfect, up-to-date order."

Cherry muttered something reassuring. She felt ashamed of her suspicions.

"While you do that," the medical secretary went on, calmly but with a catch in her voice, "I'll do another part of this deadly dull job—giving the cash fees to each doctor at the end of the day."

Mrs. Wick looked and sounded exhausted. Cherry suddenly felt tired herself. Not from her stimulating work, she knew—but from the strain of fencing with Irene Wick. And from her nerve-racking doubts.

Still, Cherry wanted to be fair and to be friends. She reached out her hand to Irene Wick, closed one of the ledgers with the other hand, and said:

"I apologize if I've said or done anything to distress you. I am really sorry. You know what, Irene? I think we've both done about all the work we can for today. Let's just do the wind-up details, and then call it a day and go home."

Mrs. Wick sighed in relief. "Yes, let's. You're right. You *are* a dear." She gave Cherry a sizing-up glance that chilled her. "Have a good weekend, Cherry."

"I hope you have a good weekend, too," Cherry replied politely, and left the office a few minutes later feeling anything but reassured.

CHAPTER VII

Sausages and Roses

A BIG EFFORT WITH MANY HELPERS—THAT WAS THE
Spencer Club's plan this weekend for getting their
summer place into shape promptly. The big push, as
Cherry said.

The four nurses had invited everyone they knew, for
Saturday or Sunday or both, offering swims, a picnic,
and some hard work. A few were scared off by chores.
Some already had made weekend plans. Two nurses at
Bertha's clinic wanted to come and bring their young
men, but had no car. They couldn't all squeeze into
Gwen's jalopy. Dr. Grey Russell offered to bring the
two couples in his car. Twelve persons promised to
come—"and that means probably nine will show up,"
Josie figured.

Cherry could not arrive at a clear-cut count of
guests. It seemed to her that people drifted end-
lessly in and out of the cottage, across the overgrown

grass—friends, neighbors, casual acquaintances—pushing a borrowed lawn mower or dragging mattresses out into the sun and air. Or repairing the barbecue grill, or hauling junk out of the distant barn, or resting under the elm trees, drinking lemonade from Bertha's Thermos jug.

Grey made a trip to the village hardware store and next time Cherry looked up, to her surprise, he was up there shingling the roof. He waved his hammer at her. Cherry had her arms full of cleaning utensils and could not wave back.

"Hi!" she called. "You're terrific! Roof surgery?"

"Just repairs," he called back. "Send Spud up to help me, hey? He offered."

Spud was Gwen's eighteen-year-old cousin from Westchester. He and his equally rotund sister, Tottie, ate constantly while they worked—gorging themselves on peanuts, candy bars, potato chips, chunks of sausage Bertha had brought—ignoring warnings from the Spencer Club about the very real health dangers of being fat. They did accomplish a great deal, though. It was Tottie's, not Spud's idea, for him to go to the local barbershop and come back clipped to the scalp. "Cool for summer."

A picnic lunch attracted two, then three, small boys and one small dog, all of whom seemed able to smell refreshments at a considerable distance. Bob Peters, the father of one boy, came to collect him and the pup, but stayed all afternoon working with Grey and the other young men in the barn.

"That's a comfortable, big barn," Grey reported. "Once the barn's cleaned up and repaired a bit, I wouldn't mind moving in there. Bachelor quarters."

The Spencer Club members looked at one another. Cherry murmured, "Why couldn't the barn be the boys' dormitory? Girls' quarters in the house. If we have overnight guests—"

"We'll need a chaperone, anyway."

"Of course."

"I think I know just the person," Cherry said. "Mrs. Faunce."

They got sidetracked by other chores. Suddenly it was late, the sun was setting, and assorted guests and helpers went home. Grey Russell was on call that night and Sunday for Dr. Fairall and Dr. Lamb and left with the others. The Spencer Club were hardly able to stay awake. Mrs. Peters, their nearest neighbor, insisted on feeding them supper. Shortly after nine o'clock, the four staggered back to their cottage, where the electricity, gas, and water were now turned on, and went to sleep.

Sunday brought sunshiny weather, a different set of visitors and neighbors, and more progress. A very shy young man who liked Josie—he had been her patient at the small hospital—arrived with his even shyer best friend. The Silent Ones, Gwen called them; otherwise, Ray and Danny. They proved to be willing marvels at cementing and carpentry repairs. Spud and Tottie returned, bringing two husky, hungry boys and swimsuits.

And later two more cars full of would-be helpers arrived. Bertha made dozens of sandwiches but their provisions ran out. Cherry had to drive to the village grocery store for more cold cuts and bread.

Their small army of helpers left the girls free to scrub and polish and plan some decorating. Bertha had been saying all day that they really should not be working on a Sunday; Sunday should be a day of religious observance and rest. However, besides the general cleanup, they urgently wanted to get ready at least two bedrooms and a crib. For Leslie and little H.J., with Mrs. Faunce as helper, were coming as soon as the Spencer Club said *Ready!*

The young couple had eagerly accepted the invitation when Cherry extended it on behalf of the Spencer Club last Friday.

"This is the best thing that's happened to us in a long time," Henry J. had said to Cherry.

He looked tired from driving a taxi all night, and taking care of his wife and infant son during the day, at hours when old Mrs. Faunce needed relief. Cherry thought they *all* needed the relief of a rest in the country, the young ballerina the most. As Henry J. said, "She hasn't really picked up, has she, Cherry?"

"No, she hasn't." Cherry looked thoughtfully at Leslie. Even sitting in a chair, languid and hollow-eyed, and bone-thin, was an effort for her. "Leslie, wouldn't you rather go back to bed?" Cherry suggested.

"I'm tired of lying down," Leslie protested. "I'm ashamed of being useless. Look at the place! Do you think we'll ever get settled? And my poor plants—" She nodded toward the several pots of greenery. "Well, at least the baby is properly cared for."

"It's a good thing he can stand my cooking," his young father said. "I can't cook very well, Cherry. Not even the baby's cereal. Mrs. Faunce can cook, but after she's done nursing and housekeeping for us, we can't ask her to cook, too."

The young couple said that if it were not for the custard, broth, and other light foods that Mrs. Wick had been bringing nearly every day, Leslie would have been poorly nourished.

"Irene Wick has been awfully nice to us," Leslie said. "She comes up several times every day—I mean, you've come every day, Cherry, and you did show Henry how to prepare the baby's bottle and cook cereal—"

"I burned the cereal," Henry J. muttered.

"That's because you tried to memorize parts of *Macbeth* while you were cooking," Leslie said.

Henry J. crouched and made a horrible, wrinkled face, fingers grasping the air. "Bubble, bubble, toil and trouble," he croaked—quoting one of *Macbeth's* three witches.

Leslie ignored him. "You know, Cherry, I'm embarrassed at Mrs. Wick's doing so much for us. She cooks, she babysits if necessary, and she insisted on brushing my hair."

"Insist!" Henry J. grunted. "She's practically managing our lives. Why, every time I look around, along comes Mrs. Irene Wick." He ran his hand angrily over his fair wavy hair. "Heck, I wish she weren't so helpful."

Henry J. stretched, then dropped to the floor and sprawled out flat on his back, with his hands under his head. "I ache," he said. "That driver's seat in the taxi is too little for me, or I'm too big for it." Lying on the floor's hard, firm surface gave his sore muscles more relief than would a soft bed or chair.

"Cherry," Leslie asked, "what are you thinking about so hard? Is anything wrong?"

"No, it's nothing." She did not know what to think of Mrs. Wick's great interest in the Youngs. "How's your bearded friend, Elijah?" Cherry asked.

"Oh, fine. He wants a taxi driver's job, too," Henry J. said.

"Well, maybe," Cherry said cautiously, "you could get him your job in case you—Did Dr. Russell have a chance to speak to you about the Stage Door?"

"About my possibly working there?...Yes, he did," Henry J. said. "The Doc is one grand guy! He's talked to his friends at the Stage Door about me, and I'm waiting to be called for an audition."

"Henry's rehearsing his original dramatic act in which he plays all four characters," Leslie said, giggling.

"I hope you can carry a tray of dishes," Cherry said with a smile. She rose to go. "Good luck! We're getting the country place ready quickly. Before you know it, Leslie, you'll be out there." Henry J. would come out on his days off from his job, whatever that turned out to be.

That was why the Spencer Club and their friends had made a concerted effort the past weekend. They accomplished their goal. Not finished, by any means—not decorated—not ready for the big party their helpers deserved—but ready enough for Leslie, little H.J., and Mrs. Faunce. Just as soon as Henry J. could borrow Elijah's station wagon, he would take his little band out there to the ocean and green country.

When Mrs. Wick heard about the forthcoming country visit, she seemed pleased for her young friends. Cherry wondered about her.

Sometimes Irene Wick's kindness wore thin. She frequently lost patience with Dr. Fairall's poorer patients—never with the rich ones, Cherry noticed. Mrs. Wick still kept their young lab technician under her thumb, saving her smiles for Dr. Fairall. "She's indispensable," he said. She had started to serve him lunch at his desk occasionally. It was a convenience to the busy man.

Cherry half expected Irene Wick to hint for a weekend invitation to the country house, but she was mistaken. The reserved Mrs. Wick kept her life outside the office private, which of course was well-advised and dignified. Not that she was secretive—she chatted with staff and sometimes patients about visiting her friends over the weekend, or flying up to Boston to see a very dear old friend. She was a widow, she said, and had no family nearer than California. It seemed to Cherry that Mrs. Wick contradicted herself, or changed details, when she repeated accounts of her weekends—as if she were lying, and did not remember her lies in detail.

"What do you know about Irene Wick?" Cherry asked Grey in confidence, at work in his office that week. "Where did she work before?"

Grey shrugged. "I don't know anything about her. Bill Fairall does—he must, because he hired her. And he relies on her without question."

"That sounds as if *you* have some question?"

"Well, not exactly, but—if I were in charge here, I'd supervise a little more. Not that I could afford the time, goodness knows. But I should. Or you should, for us, Cherry. We doctors are all so crazy busy, everything but doctoring gets neglected."

That week Cherry observed the medical secretary with particular attention. No more blank envelopes arrived. No salesmen complained. Nothing questionable happened, but Cherry, alerted, now noticed loopholes in office procedures. For example:

Miss Alice Jonas came in three times a week for an injection. The fee was ten dollars each visit. Miss Jonas paid each time in cash. Most of Dr. Lamb's elderly patients, also most of Dr. Fairall's less prosperous patients, had no checking accounts, so paid in cash. Cherry estimated about one-third paid in cash.

On Wednesday morning Mr. Xavier, an elderly patient of Dr. Fairall's, brought in one hundred dollars cash "toward Dr. Fairall's bill for his visits to me in the hospital." Cherry saw Irene Wick put it in her uniform pocket, and mark Mr. Xavier's card "Paid—$100.00," and the date.

That same Wednesday, early in the afternoon, Cherry overheard Dr. Fairall say to Irene:

"Could you run over to the bank for me before it closes? I need cash—I'll write out a check for a hundred dollars—"

And Irene Wick, with Mr. Xavier's hundred dollars in her pocket, plus Miss Jonas's ten, and very likely some more, said, "Certainly, Doctor. Here's fifty that's been paid so far today—" and she handed him that amount from her pocket.

What of the other sixty or more? Had Mrs. Wick kept it? Cherry tried to find out, without arousing the secretary's suspicions, but got nowhere.

The more Cherry thought about the hundred-dollar incident, the more concerned she became.

Why, every day it would be possible for a dishonest staff member simply to keep certain sums of cash—too small to be missed or even noticed on a daily basis, yet adding up to a considerable sum weekly. To conceal the thefts, the records could be falsified.

Or the records could simply be kept from the doctor's view! Simply evade inspection!

It was not that the doctors were careless about money; they were so busy that they *had* to rely on their staff people.

When Dr. Fairall did inquire, usually he asked the medical secretary whether that big bill for his visits to a patient in the hospital over a period of five or six weeks had been paid yet. Such a bill, including his surgeon's fee, could come to seven hundred dollars. And the dishonest staff member would not, perhaps could not, touch so noticeably large a sum.

But the doctor was not likely to remember all of the patients who visited his office during the week, nor which ones paid cash, say ten dollars three times a week for treatments. "I like to pay each time I come in," many patients said. These many smaller sums could easily be kept from the three doctors—stolen. Yes, a clever thief would be careful not to tamper with the big accounts—*and* would insist on handling all the book-keeping herself.

Was Mrs. Wick doing something like this? Had the fired nurse suspected it, too, and bluntly said so? Cherry recalled the two or three times that the name Zelda Colt had been mentioned in Mrs. Wick's presence. Each time the medical secretary had stiffened with dislike. Why had she disliked the other nurse so bitterly?

Did anyone else suspect the part-time R.N. Irene Wick? Not likely, her indifference ruled her out. And what about Dottie Nash? But the lab technician admiringly looked up to Mrs. Wick.

A tremendous sum of money flowed into the three doctors' office in a year! Cherry realized with such big sums, pilfering could go unnoticed. A skillful thief could easily go undetected for two or three years, possibly longer.

Cherry wanted to talk over this situation with someone—with Grey, or the Spencer Club nurses. Just suppose her doubts were far-fetched? The opportunity to steal, plus a few idiosyncracies, did not prove anything against Mrs. Wick.

That week seemed very long to Cherry.

Thursday was the day Henry J. planned to take Leslie, little H.J., and Mrs. Faunce to the Spencer Club's cottage.

The great day! Friend Elijah had lent his station wagon, the sun shone, and even the baby jabbered with excitement. Cherry ran upstairs just before noon, to give them a duplicate house key Gwen had had made. Henry J. was tap dancing as he carried the baby's playpen and toys to the elevator.

"Ah, the house key! Thanks, Cherry," he said. "Speaking of keys, we gave our apartment key—*one* of ours—to Mrs. Wick. She offered to come up and water Leslie's plants while we're away."

"She offered...." So it was Irene Wick's idea, Cherry thought. Well, what of it? Maybe this middle-aged woman merely needed someone—this young couple and baby—to mother and "do for."

"Tell Cherry!" Leslie called out to her husband. She and Henry J. both wore dungarees and loose sweaters. "She hasn't heard, dearest. Cherry, he starts to work Sunday at the Stage Door!"

Henry J.'s face nearly split in a smile. "Doc Grey set up an interview for me, then they saw my act and liked it."

Cherry said, "Congratulations! Cheers!"

"This job doesn't mean," Henry J. added hastily, "that I'll be an entertainer and waiter forever. I intend to go right on looking for a regular acting job, a role in a play, or whatever. Casting calls and auditions are held all summer, for fall productions." Henry J. heaved a sigh. "Anyway, for now, the Stage Door job will pay our bills. Yippee! I'm not going to drive that taxicab tonight. Goodbye, taxi."

"Then why don't you stay at the cottage until Sunday?" Cherry suggested.

He looked grateful. "Have you some chores out there for me?" Henry J. asked. "Grey told me a lot remains to be done."

"You just get your family settled, and yourself rested after the night taxi driving," Cherry said. "Thanks, anyway. Where is the Spencer Club's glamorous chaperone?"

"In here, in the bedroom—I trust you mean me," Mrs. Faunce answered. Cherry went in. The beautiful little old lady had tied a lace-trimmed apron over her dress; it made her look very slightly less the duchess than usual. "We've been packing for hours, for days, Cherry. I'm sure we're forgetting something. But what?"

No one could think what. Little H.J. gave cheerful grunts and blew a saliva bubble.

"Well, if you discover you need some last-minute thing sent to you," Cherry said, "just let Mrs. Wick or me know. There's a public telephone at the grocery store. The nearest neighbors are the Peters, and they have a phone."

Leslie suggested that they give Cherry, too, a key to their apartment. "In case Mrs. Wick isn't in the office," Leslie added.

"Leslie honey," said her husband, "you are giving the right reason instead of the true reason. Why not admit you'd rather be in touch with Cherry, because Irene Wick makes such a big production out of helping?"

"I will admit it," Leslie said calmly, "if you will admit that you'd better learn how to carry a tray of dishes. Dishes sloshing with food, my darling."

"I will admit nothing except—"

"Children, children!" Mrs. Faunce said, sounding like a fussy little bird. "We'll never get started for the country if you bicker."

"Who's bickering?" Henry J. said. "Leslie is right, having all the practical sense in this family."

"Wait until little H. J. is able to talk, you may have some surprises," Cherry said, laughing.

Leslie gave Cherry her own key to the apartment. Cherry decided it would be more tactful not to mention this fact to Irene Wick, who seemed to like, or need, to be the one most-needed person around. She resented anyone else's sharing her responsibilities and privileges. Let Irene think only she had been entrusted with the Youngs' key.

Leslie wrote down Cherry's home telephone number. "In case we need to reach you or the Spencer Club before or after office hours. About a fire or tidal wave or any emergency."

"Melodramatic, isn't she?" Mrs. Faunce said to Henry J. and led the way to the elevator. Cherry gave Leslie her arm to lean on. Henry J. scooped up the baby, saying, "Come on, fellow. Join the parade!"

And off they went to the country.

CHAPTER VIII

Grounds for Suspicion

"YES, SIR," GREY SAID TO CHERRY THAT SAME THURSDAY evening, "Henry J. was so tickled about getting a job at the Stage Door that he told me what the J. in his name stands for."

"Oh, what? Tell me!" Cherry said.

"He swore me to secrecy." Grey's calm eyes twinkled. Cherry made faces at him. "Sorry, Cherry, you're hard to resist."

She was wearing her pink dress and pink sweater. They had been to see a play performed outdoors in Central Park, this balmy June evening. Now they were in Grey's car, heading home. Cherry confessed to a worry that had bothered her through three acts:

"Did I or didn't I turn off the sterilizer in the downstairs supply room? I *think* I did. But—"

"We'll go see," Grey said. "We're not far from the offices."

On reaching the quiet moonlit street, and the brown-stone house, they were surprised to see lights on the ground floor. Who was in the office so late? It was after eleven o'clock. Grey parked the car, and they got out.

The street door was locked—"a sensible precaution at this hour," Grey said, getting out his key. He opened the door and called, "Hello!"

A startled "Hello!" answered him. Cherry heard rapid slamming of desk and file drawers. They walked into the waiting room and found Mrs. Wick, pale and frightened, leaning on her desk.

"You gave me quite a turn!" she said. "Well, I'm glad it's you and not a burglar!"

"Awfully sorry, Irene." The young doctor looked closely at her. "You *did* have a shock. Sit down."

The medical secretary was shaking. He helped her into a comfortable chair in the waiting room. Cherry brought her a glass of water. Irene Wick gratefully sipped the water. Gradually her composure returned.

"Excuse me for such silly behavior. Ordinarily I'm calm, I'm sure you both know that," Irene Wick defended herself. "Just a few nights ago there was a holdup on my street—it's a poorly lighted block. Besides that, my superintendent warned me that there had been a burglary in our apartment building. So you see why I'm nervous."

Cherry wondered whether that was the only reason for Mrs. Wick's upset on being found in the office alone.

"In that case," Grey said kindly, "you shouldn't be working so late."

"The bookkeeping had to be brought up to date!" Irene Wick said. "There's never enough time or quiet during the working day to concentrate on all the tiny details of keeping the financial records straight."

Cherry excused herself and went to see about the sterilizer. On her way to and from the supply room she walked past Irene's desk and the files. Next to Irene's typewriter were neatly addressed envelopes bearing patients' names, and neatly typed bills.

"Yes, I did turn off the sterilizer," she said to Grey and Irene Wick.

"Then let's go," Grey said. "We're taking you home, Irene."

The older woman seemed glad to have their escort. She locked the account books away for the night. Then the three of them left the brownstone house and got into Grey's car.

After a twenty-minute drive, Grey turned off at a deserted residential street. The windows in the buildings were dark; people had retired for the night. Cherry recalled reading in the newspaper that there *had* been a holdup in that street earlier in the week. Grey would not leave Cherry in the car alone, while he took Irene in.

Mrs. Wick led them to her building—a large, new, expensive one. Cherry wondered how Mrs. Wick afforded such high rent on a medical secretary's salary.

"Shall we see you safely inside your apartment door?" Grey asked. "We won't come in."

Mrs. Wick paused at the glass entrance into the lobby. Her usual look of reserve sharpened. "No, thanks, you needn't come upstairs with me." Her face, especially her pointed nose, looked pinched as if by cold. "Thanks, anyway. It's so late, you know."

It really was late, Cherry admitted. But Mrs. Wick had been concerned to keep them out. Cherry did not mention this to Grey Russell as he drove her the rest of the way home. They said good night at her door.

Cherry tiptoed into a darkened, sleeping apartment. A yawn from Gwen welcomed her into the small bedroom they shared.

"Where've you been so long?" Gwen whispered.

"Shakespeare in the park, and sleuthing," Cherry whispered back. "Go to sleep. Tell you in the morning."

The next morning Cherry woke up to hear her alarm clock and the telephone both ringing, while the Spencer Club slept peacefully on.

The phone call was for her. Henry J. was calling from Prescott, from the public telephone at the grocery store.

"I'm sorry to call so early," he said, "but I wanted to catch you before you went to work. Didn't want to interrupt your medical work."

Henry J. told Cherry that they had brought lightweight garments for little H. J., but the breeze out there was so cool that the baby needed warm clothes.

"We have him wrapped up in layers. Leslie says he looks like a fat caterpillar when he crawls," Henry J. said with a chuckle. He asked Cherry if she would please go upstairs before work, and collect some of the baby's warm sweaters, shirts, and a hood. He described where to find them. Elijah would pick them up from Cherry at midmorning. He was coming out by train to spend a few hours, and help Henry J. rehearse for his act at the Stage Door.

"I'd ask Elijah to get the things, but he has no key to our apartment, and no sense about infants," said Henry J. "And I'd rather ask you than Mrs. Wick—being a nurse you'd know better what to choose than she would. If you don't mind, Cherry—"

She did not mind in the least. Henry J. thanked her, started to hang up, then said, "Oh! In case of emergency or anything special, the Peterses said we could use their phone." He gave Cherry their number. "It's grand out here, Cherry! Leslie looks better already. See you here tomorrow, Saturday, okay?" Then he and Cherry hung up.

Cherry left for work well ahead of Josie, Bertha, and Gwen. This was partly to accommodate her six-month-old friend, partly because she had to prepare setups for patients coming in early. She reached the office so early that Irene Wick was not in yet.

"Good morning!" Cherry sang out.

Silence. No one was here. Cherry turned on the lights and air conditioning, and plumped up seat cushions in the waiting room. Then she took the elevator upstairs to the Youngs' apartment. She'd get that errand out of the way before the doctors' telephones started ringing.

It was airless in the young couple's apartment, with windows closed. But the rooms were straightened up after the disorder of departure. Cherry opened windows temporarily, and went to the chest of drawers where Henry J. said the baby's things were stored. She pulled out a center drawer, and started to select warm garments. Something fell out and fluttered to the floor. It was a bill of large denomination. Cherry dug deeper into the drawer.

She came up with a wad of money, carelessly stuffed in there. Why, there must be three to four hundred dollars here!

"How careless of Leslie and Henry J.," Cherry thought. "*If* it's theirs? Dr. Fairall believes they have almost no money at the moment. It's hard to think they would mislead him—"

Could this be Henry J.'s taxi-driving earnings? Hardly. Or had they had some last-minute windfall? There was another, very ugly possibility—Mrs. Wick could have hidden the money here, straight out of her white uniform pocket.

Wherever the money came from, Cherry decided, it had better not be left here. A closed-up apartment, no lights at night, practically signaled that this was an easy place to burglarize. And the third-floor tenants were out of town, so that at night the brownstone house stood completely dark and unguarded.

Cherry rather gingerly put the money in her handbag. She finished gathering up baby clothes, closed the windows again, and locked the Youngs' apartment door behind her. Next thing was to telephone Henry J. and ask whether she could deposit this cash for him safely in a bank, at least over the weekend.

Downstairs in the office, Cherry telephoned to the Long Island neighbors and asked Mrs. Peters, as a particular favor, to summon Henry J. and have him phone her back.

"He's here," said Mrs. Peters. "Yes, right now. He came over to return the hose we lent him yesterday."

Henry J.'s voice came out of the receiver. Cherry asked him about the money she had found. He was flabbergasted. It certainly was not his nor Leslie's, he said. . . . No, not Mrs. Faunce's, either. And Henry J. could tell Cherry no more than that. They both hung up.

Cherry thought about the persons having keys to the Youngs' apartment—herself, Mrs. Wick, and—since he owned the building—Dr. Fairall.

Dottie Nash came in at eight. Mrs. Wick had still not arrived. Not like her. . . .

Dr. Fairall came in early that morning. Cherry decided not to bother him about her find. He had just come from performing a surgery at the hospital, Cherry knew. He was thinking about lives, not money.

If that money did not belong to Dr. Fairall or the Youngs, then by logical process of elimination, the money would seem to belong to Irene Wick. But why would she want to hide or leave money in the Youngs' apartment?

Or—far-fetched but possible—had some *unknown* visitor or intruder left the money there? If so, to what purpose?

Mrs. Wick arrived at the office nearly an hour late. "I must apologize for causing you extra work, Cherry. To tell the truth I overslept."

Irene Wick hurried along with her morning duties. She showed no interest in going up to the Youngs' apartment. They all worked hard and well all morning.

Shortly before lunchtime a lull in their work occurred. Mrs. Wick said to Cherry, "I'll just run upstairs and water Leslie's plants. If that's convenient for you?" Perfectly convenient, Cherry said. With some curiosity, she watched Irene Wick go.

The medical secretary stayed upstairs for ten or fifteen minutes. Cherry visualized her watering the plants—and was Irene also searching through that tumbled drawer? Was she searching in other parts of the apartment for the missing money?

The secretary re-entered the office. Cherry watched her for any sign of nervousness, any self-betrayal. Did she look like a woman who had just discovered she'd lost several hundred dollars? Mrs. Wick was out of breath, but composed, matter-of-fact, as always.

For the next few minutes Cherry remained near Mrs. Wick and kept silent—in case Irene Wick felt moved to talk. The medical secretary did talk—about the Jensen case, and about Dottie Nash's request for certain medical supplies. Cherry felt faintly ashamed of her doubts of this hard-working woman. She said frankly to Mrs. Wick:

"This sounds extraordinary but it's true. I went up to the Youngs' apartment this morning at their request—" Mrs. Wick looked so amazed that Cherry realized she didn't know until this minute that the Youngs had given her a key to their apartment. "Well, anyway,"

Cherry said, "the important thing is this—I found nearly four hundred dollars in with little H.J.'s clothes! Is it possibly yours, Irene? Or do you know anything about it? I hope you do."

"Why, no!" Mrs. Wick said in astonishment. "Four hundred dollars! Leave it lying carelessly in a drawer? Really, Cherry! You know me better than that. Anyway, what would I be doing with such a sum? Incidentally, that cash had better be put in the bank. Right away! Can you go to the bank on lunch hour?"

"Can *you* go?" Cherry said, testing her. If the money were Mrs. Wick's, even if dishonestly acquired—

"I don't think I should touch the money. You found it," Mrs. Wick said scrupulously. "Or we could consult Dr. Fairall—and on lunch hour—"

Their eyes met and they started to laugh. Almost never did they manage a lunch hour. As a rule, lunch was a sandwich eaten while answering phones.

Mrs. Wick suggested the money be deposited in Dr. Fairall's checking account and earmarked as "Found."

"Agreed," said Cherry. "Irene, you're the one who always goes to the bank. Won't you take care of this, too?"

The medical secretary nodded.

When Irene Wick came back from the bank, she showed Cherry the doctor's bankbook and the duplicate deposit slip, proving that the found money had been deposited and earmarked.

Everything seemed to be in good order.

Except—where had that money come from? Who had hidden it?

CHAPTER IX

Dinosaur Three

THE COUNTRY PLACE WAS A GOOD DEAL LIVELIER THAT weekend with Leslie there. Every day she did a ballet dancer's limbering exercises at the porch rail. She was still weak, but already sunburned, and determined.

"I'll dance the role of the Silver Princess again before little H.J. has his first tooth!"

The baby was blooming in the country air, like one of the garden roses. He completely won over Gwen, Bertha, and Josie—so did the rest of the Young menage, including elderly Mrs. Faunce. She was delighted to act as chaperone to helpers who showed up for the weekend. Mrs. Faunce saw to it that every girl was accommodated in the house, and the boys were made comfortable in the nearly fixed-up barn. Everyone worked, played, swam. All ate hugely.

Henry J. went off to his new job in New York at the Stage Door. Little Joey Peters came over and announced it was his birthday, so the nurses gave an impromptu party, inviting the neighbors, too. Joey's mother was embarrassed but amused. Joey's father was busy with Grey and Spud, repairing stuck windows and doors. It was a happy weekend.

And yet Cherry felt as if she were watching from the sidelines, a detached observer, because her deepest attention remained fixed on something else altogether. During the next week she continued to feel the same way, moving smoothly and dreamlike through her duties, while her thoughts furiously pursued the unanswered question:

Was something going on undercover in this office? She could see bits and pieces of a situation . . .

Toward the end of the week Cherry found the note. It was one of those unbelievably busy days when all three doctors were in the office, seeing patients. A large part of New York seemed to be pouring into the brownstone all day. Cherry, Irene Wick, Rhoda Jackson, and even Dottie had all they could do to maintain a reasonably orderly flow of patients, supplies, charts, medications—to answer telephones, cope with three emergencies, soothe and reassure sick people—and prevent confusion and errors. Late in the afternoon she found evidence of somebody's slip-up.

Only this was a personal matter. Or was it?

The note was not definitely identifiable. Cherry had reached into a wastebasket at the appointment desk for a piece of scrap paper, and pulled out a nearly blank, folded, white letter, folded like an advertising letter. All that it said, in hand printing, was:

DINOSAUR THREE

"What in the world does that mean?" Cherry muttered to herself. "Dinosaur—a prehistoric animal—enormous—extinct. Is this a code?" She tried to think of equivalents or references for dinosaur, but no useful ideas emerged.

Then it occurred to Cherry that perhaps "dinosaur" in this note meant just plain old dinosaur—at the Museum of Natural History here in New York. That's it! The meeting place! Could be. And three could be the time of the meeting.

To whom was the message addressed? Who had sent it? The note gave no clue. Cherry thought of examining the envelopes in the wastebasket, to see which would fit the letter in her hand. But dozens of envelopes would fit, since business stationery was of standard size.

Try another tack. This letter had come out of the wastebasket beside Mrs. Wick's desk. Presumably the letter was for her. However, since the medical secretary opened and sifted all incoming mail for the three physicians, it was possible the note was meant for one of them. It was even possible that a patient in the waiting room had thrown away the note.

Possible, but not likely, Cherry thought.

Suppose, then, that this note making an appointment *was* for Irene Wick. At three o'clock on Monday through Friday she was working. At three o'clock on a Saturday or Sunday afternoon she would be free to go to the Museum of Natural History. Therefore, Cherry decided, the appointment was for either Saturday or Sunday.

"The Museum of Natural History is a big place," Cherry reflected. "I could go there to see who keeps this appointment, and never be noticed myself, if I'm cautious. I could go Saturday and if no meeting takes place that makes sense to me, I could try again on Sunday."

Cherry decided to disguise herself a little—just in case Mrs. Wick would be at the museum. So Cherry borrowed Gwen's reversible, thin silk rain-and-shine coat, which was navy blue on one side and beige on the other. Cherry also bought an inexpensive navy-blue silk cap, to conceal most of her hair. Irene Wick had never seen Gwen's coat and this cap.

Early Saturday afternoon at home Cherry powdered over her rosy cheeks, tucked her hair up under the cap, then put on the silk coat with the navy side out. She added a white pearl necklace and white gloves, and dark sunglasses. "I certainly don't look like my usual self," she thought. "Am I inconspicuous?" If the other nurses had not been out on Long Island, she could have checked with them.

Cherry arrived a little before three at the Museum of Natural History. She passed the bronze equestrian statue of an explorer President, climbed the great flight of stone steps, and, entering the museum, consulted a guard. He directed Cherry upstairs. In a vast hall, brimming with daylight, she found the enormous skeleton of a dinosaur. It towered over and dwarfed the hall's other exhibits, some of which were in rows and rows of glass cases. These cases afforded Cherry a fairly good hiding place and vantage point. She stationed herself near the dinosaur, head bent, pretending to read one of the several museum pamphlets she had picked up on entering.

No sign of Irene Wick! Cherry saw mostly parents and children strolling past, a few foreign visitors in native dress—no one familiar. Wait—yes, she did see someone! That red-haired man and his two young children. Wasn't he Bally, the salesman? The three were gazing up awestruck at the dinosaur.

Along came a group of Boy Scouts, and then a pretty, rather plump and bouncy, youngish woman in a flowered summer dress. She wore shoes with very high, thin heels, too thin to support her weight, so that she teetered. She stopped before the huge dinosaur and gave a pretend shudder.

"I declare, that thing gave me a turn," she said softly to no one in particular.

Bally smiled his anxious smile and mumbled something that Cherry could not hear. The woman smiled back easily and said:

"Why, yes. I'm Bunny. Are these your youngsters? Aren't they darlings!"

Bally stiffly said, "Thank you. I hope your kids are fine? Oh—er—by the way—" He swallowed hard. "Have you seen the museum pamphlet for this summer's special exhibits? I bought it because it looks so interesting."

He handed it to the pretty woman—who was only about thirty and still girlish looking. Bunny accepted the pamphlet and opened her expensive handbag. As she tucked it into the handbag, Cherry thought she saw a large white envelope extending from the pamphlet.

"I'll read it when I get home," Bunny said in a bright, artificial voice that could not have fooled anyone. "Er— do you think this hazy sky means we'll have rain?"

They discussed weather—a display of two acquaintances innocently chatting—but with such strain that they gave themselves away as strangers, Cherry thought. When they said goodbye and separated, one of the children blurted out:

"Daddy, I never saw that lady before. Not anywheres, Daddy."

That settled it. Cherry sprinted for the stairs. By the time Bunny stepped off the elevator, Cherry was waiting for her. Bunny headed for an exit, with Cherry right behind her but at a discreet distance.

Out on the street Bunny, on her stiltlike heels, clambered into a taxi. It started off through Central Park. Cherry hailed another taxi, and followed her. She had no idea who Bunny was—she did not resemble Mrs. Wick, and was about ten years younger. But she was connected with Bally, and Bally was a doubtful figure in Cherry's mind. She remembered another plain white *unaddressed* envelope that the messenger had delivered to Mrs. Wick one morning. Did such an envelope contain money—a payoff? Bunny seemed to be a go-between.

The taxi ahead left Central Park and went down Fifth Avenue. Just in case Bunny had noticed her, Cherry reversed the silk coat to its beige side, removed her sunglasses and her cap. She met the taxi driver's baffled eyes in the rear-vision mirror.

Now the taxi ahead was pulling up in front of a shop. Cherry called, "Let me out here," paid her fare in haste, and jumped out.

The taxi driver said, "You aren't the same girl who got in—"

But Cherry was already following Bunny into a shop whose windows displayed gloves, handbags, and luggage.

Fortunately the shop was large. Bunny went to the section displaying purses. Cherry took one sweeping look around, and realized that if she sat down at the glove counter, she could keep her back to Bunny and still be near enough to hear. She could recognize Bunny's voice asking a saleswoman:

"Have you a handbag in red alligator? Or red lizard? Something not too bulky, please."

"Yes, madam. We have some really beautiful imports. One moment, I will bring them to you."

Meanwhile, another salesclerk had approached Cherry, who said very softly that she was waiting for someone, and did not wish to see any gloves. The salesclerk withdrew. Then Cherry noticed a mirror reflecting another mirror that gave her a view of Bunny and the red lizard handbag she was considering buying. It was shaped like a miniature of a doctor's satchel. The red purse pleased Bunny. Cherry heard her say, "It's lovely. I'll take it."

"I know you'll enjoy using it," said Bunny's saleswoman. "This is a one-of-a-kind design, so you won't find any other woman carrying *your* handbag. Is this to be charged, madam?"

"I'll pay for it now. How much is it?"

The saleswoman named the price, nearly a hundred dollars. It left Cherry staggered. The plump, pretty woman called Bunny looked affluent but not rich. What extravagance!

Bunny, seen in the mirror, was not surprised nor appalled by the price. The saleswoman offered a pen, as if she expected the customer to pay by check. Instead, Bunny opened her handbag, took out a plain white envelope, and extracted several bills. Cherry had to tell herself *Don't stare.* Was it the same envelope Bally had slipped to her? If Bunny were only a go-between, Cherry thought, would she be spending the money from Bally? Or was Bunny a principal? Who was she in relation to Irene Wick?

"And shall we send the handbag, madam?" the saleswoman asked.

Bunny hesitated. "I *would* like to have it nicely wrapped in its own box."

"Yes, certainly. Your name and address, madam?" The saleswoman held her pencil over her salesbook.

Cherry grew tense, listening, waiting. Bunny fussed with the red handbag, making up her mind.

"I think I'll take it with me," Bunny said.

Cherry was disappointed. She had hoped to find out Bunny's last name and where she lived. Well, she'd have to keep following her. Bunny was indiscreet, she thought, to display in public this much money. A wad of money ...

Cherry remembered finding the hidden money at the Youngs' the morning after Mrs. Wick had complained of holdups and robberies in her street. Was she afraid to carry home a big sum of money? Money from her uniform pocket, patients' fees, which she had never turned over to the doctors? Afraid she, too, would be held up, or robbed?

Was this why Irene Wick used a go-between?

Suddenly, with a flutter of skirts and too-high heels, Bunny was leaving the shop. Cherry hurried out after her. Bunny, now carrying a box, was vaguely looking around as if debating where to go next. Her random gaze fell on Cherry. Did a frown of recognition—of doubt—cross the woman's face? Cherry averted her own face.

Clumsily Bunny got herself and her box into the taxi just ahead. Cherry took the next taxi and followed to Grand Central railroad station. She trailed the woman across the huge waiting room.

"I hope she goes to a ticket window," Cherry thought, "so I can stand in line behind her and hear what town she buys a ticket for."

But Bunny trotted past the ticket windows and went directly to the train gates. She went through Gate 12 and vanished down a ramp to where a train stood waiting.

Cherry could follow no farther. She did not have much money left, for one thing. More important, she wanted to complete some reports at Dr. Fairall's. Grey was to meet her there late that afternoon.

Reluctantly Cherry turned to leave. Still, she could do one thing: read the list of towns where the train departing from Gate 12 would stop. Cherry murmured the names of nearby upstate and Connecticut towns: Tarrytown, Ossining, Croton-on-Hudson, then Greenhill, Peekskill, and others.

"Too bad! A wild-goose chase." Cherry sighed, and recrossed the vast terminal. "Space enough in here for a dozen dinosaurs to roam," she thought, trying to cheer herself up.

She walked across Forty-second Street, west toward Broadway where she'd take a bus to Dr. Fairall's. Passing the stately Fifth Avenue Library Building in Bryant Park, Cherry remembered the open shelves of telephone directories from all over the United States— from all over the world. She'd bet Bunny's name and address were in there, if she only knew them!

Who was Bunny?

For that matter, who was Mrs. Irene Wick? Cherry knew nothing about her training or her record on previous jobs. She hoped Dr. Fairall knew.

On the bus she wondered what references Irene Wick had given him. Well, Irene Wick's references must have been satisfactory for Dr. Fairall to entrust his patients, the management of his office, and his financial affairs to her.

CHAPTER X

A Letter of Reference

REACHING THE BROWNSTONE, CHERRY FOUND GREY was already there. He was working alone in shirt-sleeves in the laboratory, doing his own biochemical test on a case whose progress did not satisfy him.

"Checking Dottie's findings?" Cherry asked from the doorway.

Grey looked, up, with the gas burner's flame reflected in his serious eyes. He half smiled. "Dottie's work is accurate. No, I'm exploring another diagnostic possibility. An idea Bill Fairall suggested."

"For the Matty Miller case?" This was a possible blood disorder.

"Yes. All right, I'm about finished. I've got most of the answer now, I think." Grey turned off the Bunsen burner, and with a long-handled tongs, moved the filled test tube to a wooden stand to cool. "Cherry, don't let me forget to cork this test tube before we leave here."

"Yes, Doctor. And I wish you'd give me some information."

Grey washed his hands at the lab sink, smiling over his shoulder at her and listening. As Cherry described the afternoon's events, his smile faded.

"What an ugly business," Grey said. "You be careful, Cherry. If you do any more investigating, I'm going with you."

Cherry thanked him with a look. He put on his jacket, remembered to cork the test tube, and waited for her to precede him along the hall.

"You just asked me about Mrs. Wick's references," Grey said. "I never knew about that. But I know where Bill Fairall keeps his personnel records. I don't think he'd mind if I had a look."

Grey Russell led Cherry into Dr. Fairall's office, to the bookshelves. Grey pointed behind some big reference books to a small desk-size file. It was half out of sight and had been casually left unlocked. Grey lifted out a folder marked *Wick*.

"It contains just one letter of reference," Grey said, and showed Cherry the otherwise empty folder.

"You read the letter," Cherry said. "I don't feel I have the right to."

"Well," Grey said, after reading it a minute, "this is from a woman physician Irene worked for, for seven years. It recommends Irene highly. Here, at least have a look at the letterhead."

At the top of the page was printed:
MARY LEEDS KING, M.D.
14275 Crescent Drive, Greenhill, Connecticut
Telephone: 203 Greenhill 9–7272

"Greenhill," Cherry murmured. That was one of the towns on the route Bunny had taken.

"Hmm?" Grey said. "What about Greenhill?" Cherry explained, and Grey said, "For cat's sake!"

He reached for the telephone on Dr. Fairall's desk. "Shall we dial that number and see what we can learn?"

"Wait a minute," Cherry said. "I respectfully suggest, Doctor, that we look up Dr. Mary Leeds King in the Greenhill telephone directory and in a medical directory. *Then* telephone."

"Look her up. To find out what?" Grey demanded.

"Whether Dr. Mary King exists. Or whether Irene Wick invented her. I mean, lied about her."

"But look here, Cherry, this printed stationery isn't faked—" Then Grey's face changed. "Well, yes, I see what you mean. A few dollars spent on stationery in order to make a fake reference appear authentic—"

"Exactly." Cherry said. "*Any* woman, who's in cahoots with Irene, could answer the phone and say 'Yes, this is Dr. Mary King, and I can tell you Irene Wick is a fine medical secretary.' Any woman. Maybe Bunny."

Grey stared into space somewhere over Cherry's head. "I have another idea. Let's call this number and ask for Bunny. See where that gets us."

"Right! You're a smarty!" Cherry said. "Wait—How do we know Bunny isn't Dr. King's nickname?"

"A good point," Grey said. "But we'll still want to check the directories, as you suggested."

Grey said he was for phoning now because it was still not quite five o'clock, and Dr. King might still be available for a professional call. Whereas if they delayed phoning, they could not be sure of reaching Dr. King on a Saturday evening or a Sunday. "We might only reach the answering service over the weekend," Grey pointed out.

Cherry agreed. She did not want to wait in ignorance until Monday, either.

So Dr. Grey Russell dialed 203 GR 9–7272, and handed the telephone to Cherry. Grey said under his breath, "You talk. A woman's voice could seem like one of her patients or neighbors." Cherry held the receiver end of the phone so that Grey could listen with her. They heard the phone ringing, and waited. After a long wait the faint, high voice of a child said, "H'lo?"

Cherry said, "Is Bunny there?"

"Who?" said the small voice.

"Bunny. I'd like to speak to Bunny."

A pause. "My mother isn't here now. My mother— I mean Bunny—is out."

"Oh, yes," said Cherry. She waited, to give the child time to say something more. Perhaps to ask, "Is this you, Mrs. Wick?" But that did not happen, so Cherry said, "Well, thank you very much."

"Welcome. 'Bye," and the child hung up. Cherry hung up, too. Grey shook his head.

"Dr. Mary King, huh?" he said. "Well, there's still a small chance that this *may* be her phone number. Let's go check those directories."

Cherry decided that the reports she had come here to complete could just as well wait until Monday. She went with Grey to the Fifth Avenue Library.

In the telephone directory for the Greenhill area there was no Dr. Mary Leeds King listed. There was no one named Wick listed, either.

They consulted directories of two years ago, as well as current directories, in order to give Mrs. Wick the benefit of the doubt. Still no Dr. King.

"She doesn't exist," Grey concluded, after they had spent an hour checking. "Irene Wick's reference—her one and only reference—is an outright fraud!"

The fact was baldly obvious: Bunny had posed by letter as Dr. Mary King.

"If Irene Wick got her job by lying," Cherry said to Grey, "what else won't she do, to lie and cheat?"

"She could rob us three doctors blind," Grey said. "That probably was her original intention, probably why she went to such trouble to get this job in the first place."

"But why couldn't Irene have gotten the job honestly?" Cherry asked. "She *is* a skillful, experienced medical secretary."

Grey said dryly, "Maybe she robbed her previous doctor-employers and got found out. That could be one reason why she had no honest references to show Bill Fairall."

They left the Fifth Avenue Library's marble halls and strolled in the cool greenery of Bryant Park. It was dusk; the city was growing quiet.

"*Is* Mrs. Wick stealing from us?" Grey said. "We've got to find out for sure. And prove it."

"If we knew more about Bunny, who her collaborator is—"

"Yes, that's one lead," Grey interrupted. "You and I could drive up to Greenhill tomorrow. Sunday. Want to?" Cherry nodded.

"What about that salesman Bally?" Cherry asked, and then answered herself, "We can't approach Bally. He'd only tip off Irene Wick."

"I wonder how important Bally is in this presumed racket," Grey said. "Don't you feel Irene is the key figure?"

"Yes," Cherry said. "An odd thing—Bally seems scared to death of Mrs. Wick."

They strolled for a while without saying anything. Then Grey said glumly that during the coming week at work, they would try to keep Irene Wick under surveillance.

"First thing Monday, we'd better tell Dr. Fairall everything we've learned," Grey said. "*You've* learned. Maybe he'll want to notify his lawyer, Arnold Goldsmith."

"Lawyer," Cherry repeated. She thought for a minute. "What about Dr. Fairall's accountant? Shouldn't he be notified, too? I didn't like it when Irene nearly blew up just because I offered to help her with the bookkeeping. Why is she so guarded and touchy?"

Grey had stopped stock-still in the leafy path. "My word," he said softly, "why didn't any of us realize at the time?"

Cherry raised her puzzled eyes to his. Grey explained:

"Dr. Fairall used to hire a firm of certified public accountants, CPA's, to come to the office every three months and analyze the ledgers and charge cards. The CPA's would make up a balance sheet showing our profit or loss, and they'd prepare the quarterly tax forms. *But—*"

"But what?" Cherry said.

"But Irene Wick pointed out to Dr. Fairall, after she'd been on the job for about a month, that *she* could do the quarterly audit, as a regular part of her job. Then he wouldn't have to hire the CPA's and pay their fee. I see what Irene was up to! I see! 'Saving' Dr. Fairall some money, she called it."

"This means nobody at all checks on—or even looks at—Irene's bookkeeping," Cherry said, appalled. "She could steal and steal, and nobody would ever be the wiser."

Grey nodded. "What a racket!" he said. "You know, Cherry, most medical secretaries are dedicated to their professions and to the patients. I'd as soon suspect a medical secretary as I would another doctor or a nurse. That's how Irene Wick has been able to—presumably— impose on us! She's traded on the trustworthiness, the honor of a respected profession."

Cherry smiled faintly. "In short, our Mrs. Wick who is so genteel and conscientious and takes such a pride in her work—may be a thief."

CHAPTER XI

Greenhill

CHERRY AND GREY MADE AN EARLY START ON SUNDAY morning.

"I'd rather be going in another direction, to Prescott," Cherry said to the young doctor as they drove up the Sawmill River Parkway.

"So would I," Grey said. "But this job has to be done."

Greenhill turned out to be smaller and older than Cherry had expected, with great elm trees. Homes in spacious grounds lined the main street. Grey said they should go first to the leading pharmacy in their search for information.

A traffic policeman directed them to Brown's Pharmacy. They parked in front of the county courthouse with its American flag waving in the breeze, and walked across the sunny, deserted square to a row of shops. Only a few food shops and the pharmacy were open on Sunday. Mr. Brown was there, a white-haired, pink-faced gentleman, opening up for a few hours.

"My family has run this pharmacy for three generations," he told Grey and Cherry, "and we never yet have expected our employees to work on a Sunday. What can I do for you, sir?"

"I'm Dr. Grey Russell"—the young man showed his credentials—"and this is my nurse, Cherry Ames. We need some information, Mr. Brown."

The pharmacist made a slight, respectful bow. "Glad to help you. Hope I can."

"Do you know where we can find a Dr. Mary Leeds King?" Grey asked.

"Why, pshaw, there's no Dr. King around here! Never was. What'd you say?—Mary Leeds? Never any doctor by that name, neither," said Mr. Brown. "And I've worked here since I was a boy. Maybe she's a dentist? No?...A chemist? Or a veterinarian?"

Cherry bit her lower lip to keep from laughing. Imagine Mrs. Wick's outrage if her "reference" had come from the local dog and cat doctor!

"No, no, an M.D.," Grey insisted. "Could be Dr. King isn't in Greenhill. But is she somewhere in this general area?"

Old Mr. Brown shook his head. "Doctor, I know everybody around here, and I *certainly* know the doctors because I fill the prescriptions they write, and talk to 'em on the phone. Say! Could she be an intern over at the local hospital?...No?...Well, then, there's no such doctor as Dr. Mary Leeds King, and never was!"

And never was. So Irene Wick's letter of reference was faked. Then who was Bunny, whose phone number was the reference number? And who lived—now, or two years ago—at the address printed on that faked letter?

Cherry turned to Grey. "With your permission, I'd like to ask Mr. Brown another question?" Grey nodded. "Mr. Brown, could you tell us who lives at 14275 Crescent Drive here in Greenhill?"

"Hmm." The pharmacist thought. "That's three blocks north of the traffic circle. The white brick house. That would be Mrs. Belfinger. Lydia Belfinger." He spelled the odd name for them. "And her two little girls."

To make certain they were discussing the same woman, the pharmacist described Mrs. Belfinger. He'd heard she was a widow; she had lived in Greenhill for the last two years.

Two years, Cherry thought. Mrs. Wick had been in Dr. Fairall's employ for about two years. She asked Mr. Brown if he knew anyone named Wick. He didn't.

Grey, meanwhile, had been looking at the store's telephone directory, which included several towns in this area. He reported no Wick listed, and only the one Belfinger here in Greenhill. Old Mr. Brown looked curious, but he did not ask any questions.

"If you'll look out front, Doctor, I believe that's your Mrs. Belfinger getting out of her car."

"I think it is!" Cherry exclaimed, and Grey said, "Thank you very much, Mr. Brown. You've been a great help in a professional matter."

They bustled out of the drugstore and started across the square. The woman who might be Bunny was walking away from her beautiful, expensive car. She wore sports clothes, and low-heeled shoes, without any hair showing under a kerchief. Was this woman Bunny? Then Cherry saw the woman's red lizard handbag, brand new, of unmistakable design.

"It *is* Bunny!" Cherry muttered to Grey.

They watched Bunny enter a corner bakery. She stayed ten minutes, then came out with a cakebox and bundles, and went back to her car. Grey said they could follow in his car, without Bunny's knowing it.

A few minutes later they were cruising slowly along winding, tree-shaded avenues lined with beautiful houses and gardens. "Quite impressive," Cherry said. They saw Bunny park her car in her driveway, and go into a white brick house. Grey parked just around the corner from Bunny's house. They got out, to learn what they could.

"Look," Grey said. "That woman who's cutting roses—she's a neighbor of Bunny's. We're in luck."

Admiring the roses gave Cherry and Grey a chance to speak to her. The neighbor turned out to be a pleasant, talkative woman. Grey hinted that they were house hunting. That white brick house was attractive, he remarked. Grey inquired about the neighborhood. The lady said she knew most of her neighbors. And that the resident of the white brick house was Mrs. Belfinger.

"I understand Mrs. Belfinger wasn't left much by her late husband," the neighbor said. "In fact, the realtor who rented her the house was afraid at first that she wouldn't be able to afford it, to stay on there. But then—quite suddenly—Mrs. Belfinger seemed to have plenty of money. Lots of money, for her lavish style of living! She still has. Bunny told me that she— or rather her late husband—had made some fortunate investments."

Cherry and Grey kept their faces noncommittal. Sudden and continuing wealth—did it really come from investments? Still, it was possible.

"*Very* fortunate," Cherry said to the neighbor. "Doesn't anyone else share that big house? Someone told us Mrs. Belfinger has two little girls."

"That's right," said the neighbor. "Just the three of them living there. There's a middle-aged woman who comes up to visit, occasional weekends—a woman from New York."

"Mrs. Irene Wick?" Grey asked casually.

"Why, no, I believe the name is Mrs. Ronald or Arnold, or something like that. Barbara Arnold, I think."

It could be an assumed name, Cherry thought. Trying not to sound strained, she asked, "Has she graying blond hair? A dignified woman—"

The neighbor stared down at a rosebush, trying to remember. "I'm not sure of her hair color. As for dignified, well—I suppose you could say she is. I've never seen her close up. I think this visitor wears glasses."

Irene Wick did not wear glasses.

"Or maybe I'm thinking of sunglasses?"

Grey gestured to Cherry to break away from the long-winded neighbor. By now she apparently had told them all she knew. The rest was confusion.

Grey suggested they walk to the nearest cluster of shops. "The tradespeople will know Mrs. Belfinger," he said. "Some store will be open, even on Sunday."

Two blocks away they found an attractive ice-cream shop and went in. It was deserted except for a lone clerk moping behind the soda fountain. He was about seventeen or eighteen, and looked as if he'd rather be outdoors with his friends. At least he did cheer up when Cherry and Grey sat down at the fountain, and asked him whether the shop served lunch.

"Yes, ma'am—yes, sir," the boy said. "I can serve you sandwiches, coffee, ice cream. But if you want a real experience, let me fix you each a super royal banana split."

Grey and Cherry looked at each other. Grey cautiously asked, "What's in it?"

"Everything," the boy said. "It's a masterpiece. I b'lieve you'll like it."

So they ordered it, and while the boy constructed a fantastic mound, they talked with him about this neighborhood. He was an obliging youth, willing to answer their questions. Cherry felt ashamed of pumping him for information, even though it was needed for a serious purpose.

"Oh, yes, I know Mrs. Belfinger and her two kids. Nice little kids," the boy said. He set two edible masterpieces in front of them. "Betty Lou and Janie. How they love ice cream! She brings 'em here for cones and buys ice cream to take home, too. Always vanilla," he said disgustedly.

"For the three of them?" Cherry prompted.

"Well, sometimes she has company, weekends. I can always tell when, because she buys *fancy* ice cream for company. She told me so. How do you like the—er—glop?"

Cherry could tell from his expression that Grey was not enjoying "the glop" drowned in marshmallow sauce. But he said valiantly, "Fine, fine. And has Mrs. Belfinger bought any fancy ice-cream desserts this weekend?"

"No, sir, so I guess she has no company." The boy branched off onto other subjects, useless to them.

Cherry nudged Grey and said softly, "I regret that I cannot consume another mouthful of this delicious glop. Can you?"

"No," said Grey in relief, stood up, paid, and marched out of there. Cherry stopped to compliment the boy on his creation, then followed Grey.

Although they explored Greenhill for other sources of information, by midafternoon they admitted to each other that the effort was useless. Bunny and Irene Wick's connection with her remained a question mark. Grey and Cherry drove back to New York, stymied.

That Sunday evening at home, Cherry looked in the telephone book for the address and telephone number of her predecessor. Yes, there she was, Zelda Colt, R.N., and a telephone number.

Cherry dialed the number and a woman's voice answered. "Claremont, good evening."

It took Cherry a moment to realize that this meant the Hotel Claremont, a residential hotel for women. "Miss Zelda Colt, please," she said.

"Miss Colt is out of town on vacation. She is expected back later this week," said the hotel telephone operator. "Any message?"

"Yes. Will you tell her that Cherry Ames, R.N., working for Dr. Fairall, urgently needs to talk with her?" Cherry gave her home telephone number and hung up.

It was just possible that the fired nurse knew something that no one else knew—excepting Irene.

"I just can't believe it," Dr. Fairall said to Grey and Cherry on Monday. He leaned back in his desk chair and rubbed his broad forehead. He looked hurt and shocked. "Maybe I don't *want* to believe it—not about a crackerjack medical secretary like Irene. Why, she's so close to me—so trusted—"

They had just reported to him the incidents involving Irene Wick that Cherry had witnessed since working there. The young doctor and nurse scrupulously did not make any accusations. They were leaving it to Dr. Bill Fairall to draw his own conclusions.

"Well, look," he said with a sigh. "Even though I don't doubt your word—and I'm sure Cherry's got the facts reasonably straight—you have to remember this. About two years ago, a Dr. Mary King *did* send me a long, satisfactory letter about Mrs. Wick before I hired her. And I checked with Dr. King by phone. Above all," Dr. Fairall said, "Irene has been doing a fine job for me. It's painful—and disappointing—to hear such news about her."

Dr. Fairall stared down at his hands. "Grey, are you absolutely sure of your charges against Irene?"

Grey cleared his throat. "I'm sorry to have to say this, sir. But—yes, I'm sure."

"And you, Cherry?" Dr. Fairall asked.

Cherry felt her cheeks burn. "I'm convinced—or almost—that Irene is swindling."

Dr. Fairall bounced out of his chair and paced around his office, thinking. Presently he dropped onto the leather couch. "This swindling thing makes me feel sick," he said.

"Well, speaking of feeling sick," Grey said. "Ah, you know, sir, you shouldn't eat a hasty lunch while you're working at your desk. I know it's convenient for you to have Irene serve you lunch in here, but—! Sometimes Dr. Lamb and I worry about whether you are overdoing."

Dr. Fairall gave a short laugh. "Work hard, play hard. I'm fine! Don't worry about *me*."

The phone rang. After Dr. Fairall had conferred with a hospital colleague on the telephone, he resumed with Cherry and Grey.

"Where were we? Oh, yes," Dr. Fairall said. "Well, let me say this. Your charges about Irene Wick are very serious. I wouldn't want to act in haste, though, I don't want to be unjust. And you've caught me at an extremely busy time. So—hmm—I suppose the first step would be to examine all our financial records."

Grey said, "We think you should call in an outside accountant, an auditor, and have him examine the books and charge cards."

Dr. Fairall looked at Grey. "An audit? That will take a lot of preparation, a lot of my time. And it'll cost me several hundred dollars. Still, I guess an audit is necessary in view of your charges—"

"An audit *is* necessary," Grey insisted. "You, Dr. Lamb, and I should examine our checkbooks for the last two years and *see* whether we're taking in less than we expected—Why, we haven't checked like this for a couple of years! If Irene is swindling, this affects Dr. Lamb and me, too."

"Hmm. I don't want to penalize you and Earl Lamb. Yes, we'll have to look over our checkbooks," Dr. Fairall agreed, "before we call in the auditor. All right! It's settled! I'll call him in right after we do that—and it will take time to do—and right after I've taken care of the two urgent surgeries. Macklin, and the Goucher case. Okay?"

"Fair enough," Grey said. "Meanwhile, I'll make a start on my own checkbooks. And give Dr. Lamb some help on his. There'll be a lot of old records to dig out."

"I wish we could get this matter cleared up more rapidly, in fairness to Irene," Dr. Fairall said. "But the auditing firm probably couldn't take on this job without advance notice, anyway. Well. That's it. In the meantime, we will all treat Irene as if she were innocent. Because she may well be innocent. Do you both understand?"

Grey and Cherry said Yes, they understood.

"Grey, after I do the Macklin surgery, remind me to phone the auditor."

In the next day or two Dr. Fairall was especially kind to Mrs. Wick, as if leaning over backward to be fair to her. As a result, she grew bossier than ever. Even with patients who were worried or frightened. She was anything but reassuring with a man who might become permanently disabled, with a woman whose heart condition could never get any better, only worse. Cherry intervened when she overheard Irene Wick's blunt, impatient remarks and saw the expression on the sick people's faces.

"Why, Irene," Cherry said, "I've never heard you speak to patients this way before!"

The reproof only angered Mrs. Wick. She tried to pick a quarrel with Cherry over a petty chore—who was to replace, in the examining rooms, the jars and bottles of alcohol, iodine, distilled water, and acetic acids. Cherry volunteered to do it.

As the week wore on, Grey looked more and more worried. Elderly Dr. Lamb—having been informed by Grey about the Wick situation—seemed troubled, too. What a miserable week for all of them!

Thank goodness, Cherry thought, this weekend was a long holiday: Saturday, with the fourth of July falling on Sunday, so that Independence Day would be celebrated on Monday. The entire hot, hard-working city looked forward to the three-day weekend. Cherry did, too, but with some uneasiness. For Grey had hinted about bad news.

"I'll tell you this weekend," he said. "Out at Prescott. Not here."

CHAPTER XII

A Terrible Mistake

"JULIUS!" LESLIE SHOUTED FROM THE PORCH. "DID YOU give the baby my best hair bow to play with? He's eating it! Julius, you come here—before I come after you!"

Leslie's handsome husband slipped out from behind the hydrangea bushes and made a sweeping bow—to Leslie who was pop-eyed with rage, to Elijah, to Grey and Spud, to the Spencer Club nurses who were laughing, and to the baby who seemed interested only in a passing butterfly.

"She calls me Julius when she's mad at me," Henry J. explained. "For revenge—because she knows I detest the name." He assumed a haughty British accent. "I say, my dear Leslie, I do wish you wouldn't find it necess'ry to address muh by m' middle name, doncha know?"

"Julius! So that's what the J. in Henry J. is for!" Cherry exclaimed.

In flat, ringing Nebraska accents, the ballerina in blue jeans announced, "Julius, in his case, stands for Little Caesar!"

"We, little mother," the bearded Elijah boomed, stepping forward tall and thin in his bathing shorts, "we were prophesying the future. We were foreseeing little H.J. as one day he will be!" Leslie snorted. "Verily, we tested the tyke's engineering bent by giving him your hair bow to untie. Which he chewed on."

Grey grinned and went on softly whistling. Since Russell had examined little H.J. and showed no alarm, Leslie's furious retort to Elijah was met with calm silence. Pretty soon her sputterings petered out. She joined Mrs. Faunce and the baby for a nap. The rest of the Spencer Club's Volunteer Handymen (as Grey called them) went ahead with their chores. They would go for a swim later.

The house, grounds, and barn were shaping up. With the basic cleaning and repairs done now, the Spencer Club and friends were giving the living-room walls and the dreary old furniture a fresh, clean coat of white paint. A few tables were being painted lacquer red, by Josie who loved red. Bertha had found that the old sewing machine worked, and she was making covers for seats and sofa pillows out of red-and-white-striped sailcloth. The old wooden floor was scrubbed clean and bare, not much else they could do for it. This weekend Gwen had brought along some green plants in white pots, and some striking, inexpensive Japanese paper lanterns to cover light fixtures and bare bulbs.

Now that the bushes had been pruned and the weeds pulled out of the lawn, the grounds looked neat and attractive. Some of the trees needed the care of a tree surgeon, to preserve them. The Spencer Club agreed that this was important, and was the one expense they would ask Uncle Will and Aunt Bess to pay for.

To celebrate the Fourth of July, the Spencer Club held a cookout, and invited their neighbors to join the friends who had come to help them. The brick barbecue worked fine; their big yard comfortably held people playing croquet, and swapping local news, family stories, and recipes. Dr. Lamb, his son, and daughter-in-law had promised to come but got lost on the way to Prescott. They arrived at dusk, in time to see the fireworks and the moonrise.

"A perfect Fourth," everyone said. They all were sorry when the big weekend was over.

The only flaw in that weekend for Cherry was Grey's disclosure in his car on the way home. He, Dr. Fairall, and Dr. Lamb were worried.

"Funny, we three doctors never paid much attention to business until now," Grey confided to Cherry.

He broke off talking as a car alongside unexpectedly swerved into the traffic lane just ahead of Grey. Cherry kept quiet. She wished she could see more of his profile, his expression, in the luminous dark of night and headlights.

"What's appalling," Grey said, "is that we paid almost no attention to business. The cash receipts that Irene handed us seemed about right, so we let it go at that. You know what, Cherry? We looked at our checkbooks, and found that our cash payments from patients last year and this year are lower than we expected. And now a big, sudden drop."

"How sudden? How long a period?" Cherry asked.

"Oh, in the last month or so," Grey said. "Hey! That's about how long you've been working in our office, Cherry."

"Yes.... I suppose Irene knew I was watching her? Supervising her." Grey nodded. "Could she have felt that her days on this job were numbered so she'd better steal all she dared to, in a hurry?"

"Possible." Then Grey scowled. "I wonder if Irene Wick took this job for the purpose of stealing from us doctors. The R.N. who preceded you—what's her name?—certainly didn't like Irene."

"Zelda Colt. Maybe she suspected Irene, too. That's something I want to find out."

They talked about the much needed audit. Grey said Irene Wick had been the only one to handle and see the books for two years now. Everyone else was too busy, too ignorant about bookkeeping. And if she were dishonest, *which was still not proven,* she could have falsified the books to cover up thefts. "So that the auditor will have a big, difficult job on his hands."

They were approaching Manhattan Island. First Cherry saw, across the East River, a glow thrown up into the night sky, and then—in a brilliance of millions of lights—New York's massed skyscrapers. Cherry was so excited by the spectacle that she nearly missed Grey's saying:

"Last week was the poorest week for us so far. Low earnings? Or robbed blind, last week. We've got to stop Irene right away. Tomorrow, if possible."

The workweek began on Tuesday morning, with everyone suntanned and refreshed. Including Mrs. Wick. She was full of good humor after her holiday. But when the salesman Bally dropped into the office and asked timidly if she'd enjoyed the holiday, Mrs. Wick burst out:

"Can't you stay away from here? Haven't I told you to stop bothering me? I'll phone you when we need more medications and supplies. Is that clear?"

The few patients in the waiting room stared. As Bally left, Cherry remembered the payoff envelope handed over beside the dinosaur. Whatever his sales arrangements with the medical secretary were, Mrs. Wick clearly had the upper hand.

Grey had asked Cherry to phone him on the intercom as soon as Dr. Fairall came in on Tuesday morning. He arrived about ten-thirty. Grey, coming downstairs, found him in the office area reading today's page in the appointment book. Dr. Fairall had just performed the Macklin surgery at the hospital. Though he showed the strain of two hours' delicate, difficult work, he was beaming.

"How did it go, sir?" Grey asked.

"Good! Very good! Macklin has stamina. I expect him to be able to live a normal life again."

"That's good news—and skill," Grey said admiringly. Dr. Fairall grinned, thumped Grey on the back, and said, "You'll do as well." Grey hesitated, then asked if Dr. Fairall would mind being reminded of—Grey glanced uncomfortably at Mrs. Wick who stood there at his elbow, working with an open file drawer.

"Well, of the matter we discussed last week," Grey said.

Dr. Fairall's face changed unhappily. "Oh, yes, *that.* Come in here, Grey." They went into Dr. Fairall's office, and the senior doctor closed his door.

Cherry and Irene Wick continued to work just outside his door, in the office area. They were not too busy today, even without the part-time R.N., who had left for the summer to take care of her children now on vacation from school.

Of course Cherry knew what the two doctors were talking about. Grey was reminding Dr. Fairall to call in an auditor immediately. She peered through her eyelashes at Irene Wick, sorting bills. Mrs. Wick's expression was composed, but her eyes glinted with curiosity.

"Cherry, don't you think Dr. Fairall needs a cup of black coffee, after that big job? I could bring it in to him."

Cherry answered, "I rather think he'd say so if he wanted coffee." She wondered whether Irene had overheard just now—or suspected? Cherry wondered whether her own expression was telltale.

Five minutes later Irene Wick opened Dr. Fairall's door without knocking. Had she perhaps overheard her name? Dr. Fairall crossly sent her right out. "What's he so secretive about?" Irene asked Cherry. "He never has secrets from *me*. Something's wrong."

Cherry shrugged. The morning went by without further incident.

At lunchtime Mrs. Wick served Dr. Fairall lunch in his office. That was about one o'clock

What happened next stunned Cherry.

Dr. Fairall was scheduled to leave the office at three-thirty, for a four-o'clock meeting of a medical association where he was to read a paper. At three-twenty he buzzed for Cherry to come in. She found Dr. Fairall lying on the leather couch, resting, which was unlike him. Then she saw he was pale and near collapse.

"Cherry, I don't feel right. Is Grey here?"

"Yes, Doctor, I'll call him."

Grey came downstairs on the run. When he arrived, Cherry left him alone with Dr. Fairall. She waited just outside the door in case she was needed. Mrs. Wick, she noticed, was chatting with a nervous woman patient, and seemed unaware that anything had happened to her employer. Cherry said nothing to the medical secretary. She went through the motions of deskwork until Grey called her in.

Dr. Fairall was still stretched out on the couch, breathing hard, now with his tie and collar loosened, and his shoes off. To aid circulation? Has he had a heart attack? Cherry thought. A collapse from overwork in the heat of July? Or was it—

Grey said, "Cherry, bring the stomach pump from my office. And my kit and jacket, please—I'm going home with Bill. His wife is coming with the car."

"Yes, Doctor." Then Cherry asked, "Is it food poisoning?" Grey nodded. "From lunch?"

"Yes," Grey said. Their eyes met. "Cherry, you'd better do some investigating around here."

"I certainly will!" Cherry started for the door.

"Seafood in a spicy sauce—that's what he said Irene served him for lunch." Grey snorted. "Spoiled—since it made him sick. Why, he may be acutely sick for a week!"

Cherry nodded, and went quickly for the stomach pump and other things. If Dr. Fairall were sick for a week, that could prevent calling in an auditor for a while.

When Cherry came back carrying Grey's jacket and instrument kit, she found Mrs. Wick peering into Dr. Fairall's office, shock and horror all over her face.

"It's happened!" Irene Wick whispered to Cherry. "I've asked him so often not to overwork!"

"Mmm," Cherry answered, and sped past her.

"Cherry—wait—" Mrs. Wick reached out to detain Cherry. Irene's hands shook so badly she dropped the case folder she was carrying. "Is he—Dr. Fairall—going to be all right?"

"We don't know yet," Cherry answered. "Excuse me—" and she closed the door on Irene Wick.

Cherry saw no reason to reassure the woman who might have poisoned Dr. Fairall. For food poisoning was a real and dangerous poison. If Irene Wick had served him spoiled or contaminated seafood, he could become critically ill.

Was the spoilage accidental? Or not?

To make the seafood spoiled and poisonous, Irene could simply have taken the dish out of the refrigerator in the lab, and left it standing uncovered for an hour or so—exposed outdoors in the July sun, in the backyard. The highly flavored sauce would mask any spoiled taste.

And *if* the spoilage were deliberate—? Did a delay in the audit, if she had found out about it, mean so much to Irene Wick? What did she plan to do with a few days' grace? Falsify the ledgers? Cover up traces of her stealing?

"None of this is proven," Cherry warned herself. Until and unless Irene Wick was proven guilty, she must be presumed innocent. That was the law. *"I need to find proof,"* Cherry thought.

Proof had to wait. Mrs. Fairall arrived. She, Cherry, and Grey managed to move Bill Fairall off the leather couch, down the hall—they avoided the waiting room in order not to distress any patients—out of the brownstone house, and into the car. Cherry went back to the waiting room alone, to three of Dr. Fairall's patients and two of Grey's. Fortunately, none of Dr. Lamb's patients were there today. In fairness she had to advise the five patients that she did not know how soon Dr. Fairall or Dr. Grey Russell would return. Since all of them could safely and comfortably wait several days,

Cherry suggested they make future appointments and leave now.

Next, Cherry had to deal with childishly frightened Dottie Nash. Cherry had gone into the laboratory, frankly checking the little lab refrigerator, the stove, and the few dishes for any traces of the food that Mrs. Wick had served Dr. Fairall for lunch today. No trace—no evidence—could be found. Cherry asked Dottie whether she, too, had eaten the seafood that Mrs. Wick had brought.

"No, Miss Ames. I ate a sandwich at Cob's Coffee Shop."

Cherry hunted up Irene Wick and asked, "What seafood dish did you serve Dr. Fairall today?"

"*Délices de mer*—it's a combination of crab, shrimp, and lobster in a sherry-flavored, seasoned cream sauce. I cooked it at home this morning," Irene said. "Why? I hope it didn't disagree with him."

Cherry did not answer her question, and asked, "Did you eat some for lunch today, too?"

"Why, of course. Well, only a taste, because there wasn't enough for two full portions. The only reason I didn't offer you some is because I know you prefer—"

The medical secretary went on excusing herself.

"Irene, did you bring the food in a Thermos?" Cherry asked. "I mean, from your house to here?" She had never seen a Thermos food or beverage jug here. Irene must know she could not lie on this point.

"N-no, I didn't," Irene Wick faltered. "I did pack the food carefully—practically insulated—"

"Grey says Dr. Fairall has food poisoning."

"Then it was caused by his breakfast!" Mrs. Wick exclaimed. "Or by something he ate yesterday," she insisted.

Cherry shook her head, and explained that food poisoning develops fast. Mrs. Wick's eyes shifted under Cherry's level, impersonal gaze.

"Well—then—I—I guess I've made a terrible mistake," Mrs. Wick gulped out. "I wouldn't harm Dr. Fairall for anything! You know how devoted I am—"

Maybe Irene Wick *had* made a terrible mistake. Or maybe not! One thing Cherry was sure of—that audit had to be made as promptly as possible. Secretly, without Mrs. Wick's knowing. And without Dottie's knowing, for she'd tell Mrs. Wick.

Cherry told this to Grey immediately on his return. He agreed that they could not wait until the end of that long, hot day. Together they went to call on Dr. Lamb at his apartment.

Then and there, the three of them telephoned the accounting firm that Dr. Fairall used to rely on. Grey explained the need to move with great care, so as not to arouse the medical secretary's suspicions. If alerted, she might simply vanish.

The accounting firm was willing to do the job secretly and fast. The auditor would start Friday evening after Mrs. Wick went home, and work intensively over the weekend. The auditor, with at least one assistant, would remove the charge cards, ledgers, and all other financial records to his own office, and do the job there.

They arranged that Cherry would return to the office Friday evening to admit the auditor. She'd lend him the door key, and the keys to the file cabinets and Mrs. Wick's desk. It was essential that the audit be completed, and the records back in place, before Monday morning when Mrs. Wick would come into work.

The accounting firm guaranteed to complete the audit by then. "We will telephone you on Saturday to make a progress report," the head of the accounting firm promised. "After that, we'll see."

Cherry, Grey, and old Dr. Lamb then phoned Dr. Fairall's lawyer, Arnold Goldsmith. Grey gave him a quick summary of the situation. The lawyer was concerned about Bill Fairall's illness, and eager to be of help.

"I'll be in constant touch," the lawyer promised. "I'll stay in town this weekend in case you need me. Don't worry. Good luck."

That night Cherry received a surprise telephone call. After finishing her stint at the office, and then a quick supper with Grey in a restaurant, she had returned to the Spencer Club apartment feeling quite sleepy.

"A shower and early to bed are good for that," Gwen said. But ten minutes later Gwen called Cherry out of the shower. "There's a woman on the phone named Colt or Holt, asking for you."

"Wow! Do I want to talk with her!" Cherry grabbed a towel, wrapped it and her big terry robe around her and ran, dripping, to the telephone.

"Miss Colt? . . . Hello! This is Cherry Ames."

The woman's voice reminded Cherry of a woman she had known in rural Iowa—sensible, dependable, forthright, plain, and a good person. The voice of Zelda Colt on the phone said flatly:

"I'm calling you long distance from Maine. I received your urgent message, just now, when I telephoned my hotel. We'd better not talk too long and run up a big bill. All right, Miss Ames?"

Cherry replied, "I understand, Miss Colt. But it's important to Dr. Fairall that you and I get something cleared up. I'll pay for this call—"

"Oh, are you working for Dr. Fairall? Is that Irene Wick still there?"

"Yes to both questions," Cherry said.

"Well, if that Wick woman is still there, I can guess why you left an *urgent* message for me!"

"Yes? . . . Did you have any difficulty with Mrs. Wick?" Cherry asked.

"Don't you?" Miss Colt demanded. Then Cherry heard her sigh. "She cost me my job, Miss Ames. I don't know what she said about me to Dr. Fairall—she must have told some lie—because before she came, Doctor relied on me. He knew I did my best—for him, for the patients—always—"

That voice didn't suggest someone callous who'd refuse to help a sick or disabled person with a dress or a shoe.

"I'm sorry if you had an unfortunate experience," Cherry said. If she could, she'd like to clear Nurse

Zelda Colt's reputation with Dr. Fairall. "I hope you're in a happier situation now, Miss Colt."

"Oh, yes! I'm working for a fine young doctor in New York, an internist—" Miss Colt gave his name, which Cherry recognized. "Also I have a job offer from"—she named a leading hospital—"on the basis of my earlier references."

Well, Miss Colt must be a good nurse with decent attitudes, Cherry thought. The medical secretary *had* lied!

As tactfully as possible, she told Miss Colt that she needed whatever information the nurse could give her about Irene Wick.

"You don't trust her, do you?" said the nurse. "Neither did I. Couldn't prove anything, but I noticed—well, too many tricky little practices. You know what I mean?" Cherry said Yes, and then inquired if Miss Colt knew anything about a woman named Bunny. "Bunny?...No.... And how Irene Wick honeys up to the doctor!"

They agreed that Dr. Fairall was brilliant and a dynamo, but in some ways an impractical man. He was too dedicated a doctor to mistrust other medical personnel.

"Does he still work so hard?" Miss Colt asked. "And go in for so many outside interests?"

Cherry said, "Yes, but now he isn't well—"

"I'm not surprised to hear it!" Miss Colt interrupted. "He had a breakdown—exhaustion—once while I worked for him. He went away for periodic rests. And in the emergency he did the most awful thing! So Irene could keep his business moving, she said. Miss Ames, you pay attention to this! Dr. Fairall gave Irene Wick power of attorney—power to write letters and checks, and sign his name to them! She may still have power of attorney!"

Cherry caught her breath. "You mean Mrs. Wick may be able to draw on his checking account?"

That was exactly what Zelda Colt meant, and was worried about. Because, she said, she had always had a strong suspicion that Mrs. Wick was stealing from Dr. Fairall—"and stealing from Dr. Lamb and a young relief doctor, too. I never found out just how she worked it. But I suspected that was why she was so eager to get rid of the outside accountant firm, and handle the bookkeeping all by herself."

Cherry relayed this information in person, privately to Grey. He relayed it to Dr. Fairall's lawyer and to the certified public accountants. To do so, Grey left the office and used a public telephone blocks away. This was done the next morning, Wednesday.

Early that evening Grey and Cherry left the brownstone house separately, for Mrs. Wick's benefit. They met half an hour later at the lawyer's office in another part of the city.

The lawyer, Arnold Goldsmith, was a tall, lean man with prematurely white hair. As he ushered them in, he asked Grey with concern, "How's Bill Fairall now?"

Grey was able to report that Dr. Fairall was much better—still miserably sick with food poisoning, but not in danger. The lawyer said that if Mrs. Wick had deliberately poisoned Dr. Fairall she should be prosecuted. But how would they ever be able to prove it was anything but what Mrs. Wick had called it—"a terrible mistake"? Impossible.

"Well, now, Miss Ames, Dr. Russell—you want advice and possibly action from me, but you haven't consulted Dr. Fairall first. I don't like that."

"Only because Dr. Fairall is too sick to be consulted." Cherry was glad the lawyer was conscientious.

"All right," the lawyer said. "Suppose you give me the facts."

So they told him about Mrs. Wick's suspected stealing, and her suspected graft from Bally. Assuring the lawyer they could provide details later, they came to the immediately urgent fact: Mrs. Wick might still have power of attorney for Dr. Fairall.

"If she has it, I'm afraid she might misuse this power now that Dr. Fairall is sick," Cherry said. "Maybe make one last, big haul. What's to prevent Mrs. Wick from writing and signing a big check, made out to cash, drawn on Dr. Fairall's account—say, for several thousand dollars? Or everything the doctor has in the accounts? Then she could simply vanish."

Grey nodded in agreement. But Arnold Goldsmith said, "An employer entrusts an employee with power of attorney for an essential reason—to keep the business running in his absence. Surely Dr. Fairall wouldn't turn over his checkbook and bankbooks to just anybody."

"Mrs. Wick's references are open to question," Grey said.

The lawyer frowned. "That's not so good. Hmm."

He asked them several questions, which they answered.

"Well," the lawyer said at last, "the thefts are presumed, not proven until the auditor's report is made. We have to wait for the auditor's report before we can accuse that medical secretary—even indirectly. All we can do is wait. And keep your mouths shut around that Mrs. Wick!"

By Saturday night they had their answer.

First, Cherry had made sure before the weekend started that Mrs. Wick would not stay to work alone on Friday evening, nor come in on Saturday. "Oh, no," Irene Wick had assured her. "I'm spending this weekend with a friend upstate."

So the auditor and his assistant had executed their plan.

Saturday evening the auditor telephoned Cherry and Grey at the Spencer Club apartment. Grey was eating supper with her there, and of all people, Spud and Tottie. They had come into the city to shop.

The lawyer, Mr. Goldsmith, was also staying home this hot Saturday evening, waiting for the auditor's telephone call.

The auditor reported, "Your medical secretary has been stealing systematically for the past two years. She never turned over to the doctors the whole amount of what the patients paid her in cash. I'd estimate that she kept as much as two hundred dollars a week—every week—for two years.

"And we can prove our charges in two ways," the auditor said. "First, the cash deposits in the doctors' bank accounts were far too small. The doctors trusted the secretary to put the patients' cash payments in the bank, but she put in only what she didn't keep.

"Second, we've found discrepancies in the records—"

Cherry interrupted to ask, "Didn't Mrs. Wick falsify the records?"

"She started to, but didn't keep it up," the auditor said. "Apparently it was too much work for her. We did find a few rigged entries freshly written in, as if she tried again recently." Cherry thought of the evening she and Grey had unexpectedly gone to the office, and found Mrs. Wick working on the books.

The auditor went on, "As I say, we found glaring discrepancies between the charge cards and the ledgers. We found discrepancies between the figures in the appointment books, where the doctors wrote down each fee, and the ledgers. Her bookkeeping is in such a mess that it's hard to—Well, just let me say we have absolute proof of Mrs. Wick's thefts. We estimate she stole about twenty thousand dollars."

When Cherry recovered, she asked, "What about kickbacks she probably received from Bally, that salesman she favored?"

The auditor suggested that this matter be left to the lawyer and the police.

The auditor arranged with Grey and Cherry to return the records to the brownstone house Sunday at noon, keeping the records in their original order.

Grey and Cherry had been listening on the phone together. Their guests, Spud and Tottie, had grown bored and left. Just as well, since these conversations were confidential.

Grey, after thinking it over, notified Dr. Lamb by telephone of the auditor's findings. The old man was not, as Grey had feared, upset. He even took the news with a joke, and told Grey:

"Go ahead and catch her! Anything you do in that regard is all right with me.... Say, Grey, have you seen my whatchamacallit? Think Mrs. Wick stole it, too?"

~~~~~~

CHAPTER XIII

The Red Purse

THE SPENCER CLUB'S TELEPHONE RANG INSISTENTLY. IT was seven A.M. that hot Monday morning, July twelfth. Cherry woke up and staggered to the telephone. The call was for her, as she'd half expected—from the lawyer.

"Sorry to disturb you, Miss Ames," he said. "I'm going to call Dr. Fairall's bank as soon as it opens, and warn them to be on the lookout for Irene Wick. In case she tries to withdraw any money from the doctor's account, or tries—in any bank—to cash a check she's written herself with Fairall's power of attorney—well, she could be arrested on the spot."

It was a trap for Mrs. Wick, as well as a safeguard for Dr. Fairall. "But suppose," Cherry asked, "that Mrs. Wick is too wary even to report for work this morning?"

Mr. Goldsmith said, "In that case we'd have a harder time to catch her. But you've all moved with complete secrecy in making this audit. So I'd say Mrs. Wick doesn't suspect it's been made, or even suspect that it might be made in the future. If she did—If she'd been alerted—she'd have disappeared right after Dr. Fairall got sick."

"Then you don't believe Irene Wick deliberately poisoned him?" Cherry asked.

"No, I don't," the lawyer said. "I think the food spoilage was an accident. You've read too much into that, Miss Ames. A red herring," the lawyer said dryly. "No, Irene Wick didn't suspect about the audit, she didn't poison Dr. Fairall on purpose, she still feels confident that she's safe to pursue her racket. You'll see, she'll come to work today."

The lawyer added, "Wait—one more thing, Miss Ames. Last week I talked with the officer at Dr. Fairall's bank. He let me know—reluctantly, I must say!—that Mrs. Wick has her own small checking account at their bank, and rents a safe-deposit box."

"A handy place to keep the cash she steals?" Cherry suggested.

"She probably keeps it there, temporarily. And keeps it elsewhere, too, I should think. Still," Mr. Goldsmith said, "I'm not yet ready to call in the police. Publicity of this sort might hurt Dr. Fairall—his patients might doubt his judgment in other matters. Miss Ames, I'm going to stay in my office all morning, in case you or Dr. Russell need me." The lawyer hung up.

Irene Wick did come to work that morning, early and brisk as usual. She looked sunburned after her weekend away. With her white linen suit she carried a red lizard handbag of distinctive design.

"What a handsome new handbag!" Cherry said. She was positive she recognized it as the one-of-a-kind purse Bunny had purchased at the Fifth Avenue shop. She tried not to stare at it.

"Thank you," Irene Wick said. She opened the bag to show Cherry its fine lining, and Cherry saw the label. Yes, the same shop. So there *was* a connection between Bunny and Irene Wick!

"It is a handsome bag, isn't it?" Mrs. Wick said. "It's a present—my hostess this weekend insisted on giving it to me. She's carried it a few times, but it really is new."

"What a nice hostess!" Cherry commented.

Mrs. Wick smiled and said, "You're here early." She began pulling off her gloves when she frowned, then walked over to the desk and cautiously placed her hand on the appointment book. It was closed. Usually it lay open. *Closed!* Mrs. Wick's color changed beneath her suntan.

"Didn't I leave the appointment book open to today's date before I left here on Friday afternoon?" she muttered. "Didn't I—I always do—" Her trembling voice broke off.

Cherry said quickly, "Oh, I did that—I moved it to dust a little just now." She began to tremble and gripped her hands together to stop it.

For she had slipped up in not returning the appointment book to exactly its usual position. Mrs. Wick was so fussy and rigid in her methods that she noticed the most petty change. Cherry hoped that the auditor and his assistant had managed to keep ledgers, charge cards, bills, and canceled checks in their original order.

As far as Cherry could see, they had. Cherry and Grey had been there yesterday when Mr. Curtis and Mr. Joseph had returned the big load of records. Then Cherry had made a particular effort, checking through all the records for two hours, to see that they *were* in the usual order. Only then had she locked the files and desk.

Now Cherry held her breath. "I'm not as eagle-eyed with paperwork as a secretary is," Cherry thought. "If I overlooked opening the appointment book, maybe I've made a mistake on some other detail, too."

Mrs. Wick said sharply, "Well, I wish you would leave things in proper order, Cherry. Anyway, Winnie is supposed to come in to clean, not you. Not the nurse." This extra little stab of sarcasm seemed to relieve and calm Irene Wick. She asked, "How is Dr. Fairall? When did Grey last see him?"

Cherry told her Grey had seen Dr. Fairall yesterday, and he was much better. The telephone rang, today's first patient calling. Mrs. Wick answered. The intercom buzzed. Grey had a minor emergency case coming in, he said. He wanted Cherry to set up a treatment room, right away.

"Emergency arriving," Cherry said to Irene. "Dr. Russell says home accident. I'll be back in about ten minutes, Irene."

Ten minutes later Cherry came back into the waiting room and office area. Mrs. Wick was not around. A file drawer full of charge cards stood open. Cherry frowned. It was not like Irene Wick to leave the telephones unattended. Nor to leave a file drawer open. Cherry looked into the file drawer—and saw that half of the cards were upside down.

Had they been upside down yesterday? Or was this a signal from Irene Wick saying, in effect, "I see my records have been tampered with. I have always feared an auditor was to have been called in, and now apparently he has been—and has examined these records."

Or was the upside-down placing simply a routine way of not losing one's place when working with a mass of cards? Had Mrs. Wick merely gone to change into uniform? Or was she setting out supplies?

Cherry took the telephone calls alone for a while. When Dottie Nash came in, Cherry put her in charge of the phones, and went to search the street floor. Irene Wick was not in any of these rooms. Cherry ran upstairs to the second floor, looking into each empty room. In the dressing room, her own and Irene's white uniforms still hung on the rack. But Irene's hat, gloves, and red purse were not there.

Cherry knocked, then looked into Grey's office. No Irene. Grey glanced up inquiringly.

"Have you seen Mrs. Wick?" He shook his head. "Then she's gone—run away."

"Are you sure?"

"Well, she left a file drawer standing open—she never does that—she must've seen—"

Grey pressed an intercom button and asked Dottie Nash for Mrs. Wick.

"She went home about ten minutes ago. Said she didn't feel well," Dottie replied. "Can I do something for you, Dr. Russell?"

"No, thanks—yes. Give me Mrs. Wick's home phone number, please." Grey scribbled it down. "Thanks, Dottie. Now will you get this number for me?"

It was the lawyer's number. Because Dottie might listen in, and might still be in touch with Mrs. Wick to warn her, they could not now make arrangements by phone. At the other end a woman's voice answered by stating the phone number. Then Grey said casually into the phone:

"Arnold? . . . Good morning. . . . This is Dr. Russell. Feeling better? . . . Can you come in to let me look you over? . . . Yes, can do. . . . Why, yes. . . . Take the elevator to the second floor. And you remember my office is at the far end of the hall."

The instant Grey hung up, Cherry turned off the intercom, so Dottie could not hear.

"Arnold Goldsmith will be right over," Grey said to Cherry. "Listen—about this emergency patient—and our other patients today—the lawyer hinted that he wants us to go with him, I assume to locate Irene Wick. . . . Yes, both of us, Cherry. So I'm going to phone Dr. Lamb to come in. We'll have to get a relief nurse. Do you know an R.N. who's available?"

Cherry shook her head. The shortage of nurses, and of doctors too, was a serious problem. Women were urgently needed in both skills.

"Unless," Cherry said, "Zelda Colt is back in New York from vacation but not yet back on her job. She knows Dr. Lamb and some of the patients, and the setup here."

"It's worth a try," Grey said.

He sent Cherry out of the building to telephone Miss Colt, and also Irene Wick's apartment. No one answered there, though Cherry rang several times, before and after calling Zelda Colt. By good luck, Miss Colt was available, and more than willing to help out "—even though I'll have to work with Irene Wick."

"Mrs. Wick is—er—out sick today," Cherry said. "There'll be just you, Dottie, and Dr. Lamb. I'll explain later, Miss Colt. This is an emergency. Thank you ever so much."

"Thank *you*," the other nurse said. "This gives me back my good reputation at Dr. Fairall's. I'll come right over. 'Bye now."

Cherry sped back to the office, stopping briefly to check with Dottie. The young woman was rather upset at being left alone and in charge. Cherry reassured her, told her that Zelda Colt and Dr. Lamb were coming, and learned that not many patients had called in so far. Dottie said Dr. Russell was treating the accident case—removing a glass splinter from a woman's hand. Cherry started upstairs to help bandage the hand, but met the woman already leaving, stepping out of the elevator. At the same time, the lawyer arrived. He and Cherry went up to Grey's office together.

Arnold Goldsmith took hold of the situation with an iron grip, to Cherry's relief. First he listened to her hasty report about the red handbag, the file drawer left open, the unanswered telephone in Irene Wick's apartment.

"She isn't there," the lawyer said. "I sent a man from my office to her apartment building right after you phoned me, Grey. He persuaded the superintendent to let him in. Not there. By the way, her clothes are still there. She didn't plan this disappearance. The audit took her by surprise. Now she knows the racket is over. Well! We'll have to surprise her again, with an arrest."

The lawyer already had checked with the bank, to learn whether Irene Wick had gone there that morning. But Mrs. Wick was too foxy for that. After she'd seen the closed appointment book, and the possibly disarranged charge cards, she must have felt the trap closing in around her.

The lawyer figured Mrs. Wick would flee to her accomplice, Bunny, in Greenhill. Last week he had sent an investigator there, who discovered that Mrs. Lydia Belfinger had a very large bank account in Greenhill. The account was jointly held with a Mrs. I. W. Sproull— "and you can be sure that's Irene Wick. Wick is probably her maiden name." Possibly even more significant, the two women also rented a safe-deposit box—the largest size—in the Greenhill bank. So Irene Wick would want to pull out the money in that account, and the money that very likely was in that safe-deposit box, before she fled Greenhill and hid from arrest.

"Does she own a car?" the lawyer asked Grey and Cherry. "No?...Then wouldn't she go to Greenhill by train? Just on an off chance I've sent another investigator to watch for her at the train gate at Grand Central, and try to detain her. But—" Arnold Goldsmith shrugged. "I haven't heard from him. Anyway, she has a head start on us. Can you come now? My car's outside. We'd better get to Bunny's house quickly—or Irene Wick and the money will be gone."

"We'll come, of course," Grey said, "but why?"

"I need you both," Arnold Goldsmith said. "Explain on the way up there."

Just before they left the brownstone, Dottie Nash came running after Cherry, almost in tears. Cherry kept walking and listened.

"Cherry, Zelda Colt is here, as you told me—and how glad I am to see her! She's always nice to me. But what's happening with Mrs. Wick? I do admire her—even if she was furious when I—when I—"

"When you what?" Cherry encouraged Dottie.

"When I borrowed, just for overnight, fifteen dollars from what old Mrs. Morris paid in cash, so I could buy that blue dress for a party I was going to. I swear I returned the fifteen dollars right away, but Mrs. Wick said I'd *stolen* it, and if I ever took any money around here again, she'd have me fired just like she got rid of Miss Colt!"

Cherry called to the beckoning lawyer, "I'm coming! ... Dottie, listen to me. You were foolish, you did the wrong thing, but *you* weren't as dishonest as Mrs. Wick. Have to go now!"

They drove to Greenhill. It was a hard, fast drive—Cherry did not enjoy it. The lawyer, driving, briefed them:

He hoped Cherry could persuade Irene Wick to submit peaceably to arrest, to cooperate by surrendering the stolen money, and telling her full story. "She might not listen to me," Arnold Goldsmith said. "She's never seen me before. She'll think of me only as a prosecutor." The lawyer also needed Grey and Cherry to identify Irene and Bunny, since he had only descriptions and had never seen the two women. He had particular need of Grey.

"There are two legal methods to arrest Irene and Bunny," the lawyer explained. "Either we must go before the local magistrate—he's probably in the Greenhill courthouse. Or rather, Grey will go before the magistrate, because Irene has stolen from Grey. Grey, as witness, will give his story to the magistrate in the form of a sworn statement. On the basis of Grey's affidavit, the magistrate will issue an arrest warrant to the local police officer. Then the police officer will go to Bunny's house, we with him, and he will arrest Irene and Bunny—using force if necessary—"

Grey interrupted to ask, "What about getting a search warrant to enter Bunny's house?"

"If we, or rather the police officer, has an arrest warrant," Arnold Goldsmith said, "we don't need a search warrant. The policeman has a right to search the house *incident to* the arrest. But! This method—getting an arrest warrant—takes time."

Cherry sighed. "Irene and Bunny could be on a plane by that time."

"Exactly," the lawyer said. "So I propose that Grey use the other, less usual method. You know, it's possible to make a private citizen's arrest."

"I've heard of that," Grey said, "but precisely what is it?"

"Well a private citizen may arrest the wrongdoer— but only for a felony that has actually been committed. Irene Wick's stealing in large amounts is certainly a felony. And we are sure she stole, and sure that Bunny aided her, either as accomplice or accessory after the fact. So I would advise you, Grey, to make a private arrest of Irene Wick and Bunny. I'll help you, of course. And I'll help when you bring them before the local magistrate, where they may be jailed or arrange bail."

Grey grumbled about this distasteful assignment, but he agreed to act on behalf of Dr. Fairall, Dr. Lamb, and himself.

They reached the quiet town late in the morning. They drove through the square past Brown's Pharmacy, into the residential area, past the ice-cream shop, and then almost to Mrs. Belfinger's handsome white brick house. They parked around the corner, half concealed by a high hedge. The lawyer whistled when he saw the house and its grounds. Bunny's expensive car stood in the driveway.

"So that's how the two women have been spending Dr. Fairall's patients' fees," Arnold Goldsmith said. "And your earnings, Grey, and Dr. Lamb's. Now! How are we going to gain entry into that house?"

"Look," Cherry said. From their car they watched Bunny, plump and puffing, come out of the house, carrying a big, heavy suitcase, and put it into the white car. Bunny's hair was disheveled, and she wore sloppy bedroom slippers; otherwise she was neatly dressed in a silk suit and earrings, as if almost ready to leave. Bunny hurried back into the house, leaving the front door open.

"Maybe Irene Wick will come out next with her suitcase," Grey muttered. "She can't see us."

"*Maybe* isn't good enough," Arnold Goldsmith said. "We're going in there. Now. Be quick!"

They slid out of their car, walked around the corner, came out from behind the concealing hedge, and ran up the walk of the white brick house. To Cherry that flagstone walk seemed miles long as she ran, and she hated what she was doing. Had to do. She noticed that the tall, dense hedge enclosed this entire property, like a wall. Bunny called out in confusion: "Who's there?" The three of them gained the porch just as Bunny started to close the house door. The lawyer walked in anyway, saying, "Mrs. Belfinger, I *must* see you! I'm sorry, but I must!" Cherry and Grey followed him into an entrance hall.

"Who are you? Get out of my house—all three of you!" Bunny screamed. "I'll call the police!"

"I wish you would," Arnold Goldsmith said. "Mrs. Belfinger, I am a lawyer, and this is Dr. Grey Russell from whom you stole, or at least whose stolen money you received—"

"Get out! Get out! I don't know any of you!" Bunny's pretty, plump face crumpled and she started childishly to cry.

Grey looked as embarrassed and disgusted as Cherry felt. None of them felt any sentimentality for thieves. "Mrs. Belfinger, I am here to arrest you and Irene Wick," he said. "And I'm here to get back money stolen from two other doctors and myself—"

Bunny drowned Grey out when he said the word "stolen." "I am not a thief!" she shouted. "I don't know anything about you and your silly money!"

"Mrs. Belfinger, as a citizen I arrest you for felony," Grey said. He took hold gently of her arm. "Where is Irene—"

"Don't you dare touch me!" Bunny screamed. She broke free and lunged toward the open front door. But Cherry stamped hard on Bunny's foot, and Bunny in pain and surprise stopped and just stood there. The lawyer looked at Cherry with astonishment, then admiration. He said:

"Mrs. Belfinger, stop that sniffling and tell us where Irene Wick is."

Bunny wiped her eyes and sulked. "I don't know anyone of that name," she loftily informed the lawyer.

"You're Irene Wick's accomplice," Cherry said. "I'm Dr. Fairall's nurse and I found the 'Dinosaur Three' note in the wastebasket at her desk. I saw you meet Bally in the museum. I saw you accept money from him—" Bunny's face froze into a blank stare. "I saw you," Cherry persisted, "buy a red lizard handbag. And I saw Irene Wick carry that red handbag—you gave it to her this weekend."

"You're lying," Bunny spat at Cherry. "You didn't see any such things! Lies! Lies!"

Cherry said, "I see something interesting in the living room," and went in there. The two men followed, shepherding Bunny. Cherry thought she heard a door close softly somewhere—it sounded like a closet door or room door—but she could not be sure. Arnold Goldsmith heard it, too, for he lifted his eaglelike head. He stationed himself in the open archway between living room and entrance hall, where he could watch the entrance door and the driveway. Anyone entering or leaving these hedged-in grounds would have to pass along the driveway.

The living room was richly furnished. What had caught Cherry's eye was an open suitcase on the floor, carelessly filled with a silver coffee service and silver flatware, as if being packed in haste. Cherry noticed a woman's pink coat lying on a sofa. The weather was too warm for a coat—unless one were going on a trip to a cool climate. Cherry picked up the coat. Under it lay a small car case and a second woman's coat, of conservative tan—for a taller woman than Bunny. For someone of Irene Wick's size.

Cherry put down the coats and looked squarely at Bunny. "Where is she?"

"If Mrs. Wick will cooperate with us and with the police," the lawyer said, loudly enough to be heard in other rooms, "you both will get off more easily."

Only silence answered the lawyer. Then footsteps sounded on the porch. The doorbell rang. A young woman's cheerful voice—not Mrs. Wick's voice— called out:

"Hi, Bunny! Here are your kids back from playing at our house!"

Grey prodded Bunny. She called out:

"Thank you, Jean. I—I'm—Excuse me, but I can't ask you in—"

Arnold Goldsmith, standing near the house door, nodded to the woman. He murmured, "A little difficulty, unfortunately." Cherry had a glimpse of the neighbor and of two small girls with her.

"Oh." The neighbor looked curiously at Mr. Goldsmith, then said, "Sorry I barged in at an awkward time! I'll see you later, Bunny."

Grey prodded Bunny, who answered nervously. "Yes. Oh, yes, Jean."

"By the way, Bunny," the neighbor called, "I hope nothing serious is wrong?"

Bunny went white. "Oh, no. Nothing much."

"Then why," the neighbor called, "did your sister leave last night for New York, and then come right back here this morning?"

So Irene Wick was Bunny's sister!

The lawyer stepped forward toward the neighbor. "Excuse us, madam, you may see your friend later.

We have an emergency to take care of now, I'm afraid. Come in, children," he said gently, "come in."

The neighbor muttered something and went away. Arnold Goldsmith stood aside and smiled at the two little girls who uncertainly came into the living room.

Round-faced and brown-haired like Bunny, they were about four and six years old. They wore blue play dresses and red shoes. Cherry felt sorry for them. She said impulsively:

"What dear children! Won't you tell us their names, Mrs. Belfinger?" Cherry knew it was important not to frighten these little ones.

"Betty Lou is my big girl," Bunny said tonelessly, "and Janie is my little girl."

The visitors smiled and said hello. The two little girls looked solemnly back at them. The older child asked, "Mommy, who are these people?"

Bunny hesitated. "Tell you later. Are you hungry?" The children nodded.

Cherry called, "Irene, come out! If you care anything for Bunny and her children, come out!"

Someone moved, somewhere in the house. Grey pointed to a telephone on a coffee table. The lawyer nodded and said, "Call the police now." Both little girls started to cry. Grey let their mother go to comfort them, as he unhappily telephoned.

Suddenly someone ran through the entrance hall, flashing past the lawyer. A flash of something red, too—He reached for, but could not catch Irene Wick who flew out across the porch. She raced down the porch steps, but by now, Cherry was running after her. Irene Wick pounded along the driveway, heading for the car. She called out:

"Bunny! Bunny! You'll be all right! I'll—come back for—you—later—"

Cherry ran headlong, blindly, slamming into Irene Wick just as she reached the white car. Cherry was going at such speed that it threw her hard against Mrs. Wick, and they both fell against the side of the car, then toppled to the ground.

"—come back for you and the children!" Irene Wick was still screaming. She clawed furiously at Cherry's face, scratching with her nails.

Cherry grabbed the woman's wrists, and struggling, forced Irene's arms slowly down to her sides. Cherry pinned her to the ground. Irene Wick was scratching and biting when Grey came to rescue her.

"You vicious woman!" Cherry gasped. She climbed to her feet. She felt blood on her scratched face, and her shoulder was sore—wrenched. Never mind—the main thing was that Grey had Irene on her feet away from the car, in his grip.

The red purse lay in the driveway. Cherry picked it up. Mrs. Wick was limping into the house in Grey's custody. Cherry first looked into the white car, and saw that the car keys were there. Then she followed into the house, bringing the red purse.

The lawyer was saying to Bunny, "The nurse, not you, will feed the children, Mrs. Belfinger. You're staying on that chair where I can watch you."

He asked Cherry to take Betty Lou and Janie across the hall into the dining room and serve them lunch, which their mother said was ready in the refrigerator. The frightened children did not want to leave the living room and their mother. Cherry gently coaxed them, and Bunny said, "Be good girls and go with the nurse."

"Are you really and truly a nurse?" Betty Lou asked, round-eyed. Cherry nodded. "Then where's your white dress and white cap?"

Janie answered scornfully, "In the laundry. Or she left it home. Come on, I'm hungry."

So Cherry fed the children. She felt deeply sorry for them, and tried to calm them and reassure them, telling stories and jokes and a puzzle. When she heard the police car arrive, she shut the dining-room door. Where would the children go, if their mother as well as Irene Wick received a prison sentence? Who would take care of them? Cherry hoped the court would be merciful.

"More milk, Janie? Betty Lou? There's one more cookie with your name on it."

Betty Lou studied the last cookie. "Where's my name on it?"

Harsh sounds of whimpering came from the other room against calm, male voices. Cherry heard Irene Wick cry out, "It's a relief to tell! I've been under such a strain—!" Then came Bunny's softer voice, saying something quiet, resigned, and undistinguishable.

Grey came into the dining room. "Cherry, the lawyer and the police officers and I are taking—I mean, going with Irene and Bunny to—" He glanced at the children. Betty Lou, at six, might be able to gather that he meant *to the magistrate, to jail*.

"Yes, I understand," Cherry said.

"Will you stay here with these two pretty girls?" Grey smiled at the children, who trustfully smiled back at him.

"Of course I'll stay," Cherry said. "We're right in the middle of a story."

"Their mother says Mattie, the day maid, will be here soon. But you stay until—until arrangements are made, will you? I'll come back for you as soon as I can."

And Grey left, closing the door behind him.

Cherry kept the two little girls with her in the closed-off dining room. Through the windows and trees she saw a police car drive away. Mrs. Wick and Grey were in it. The lawyer drove off in his car with Bunny and another police officer. Once more the house grew quiet.

"Where's Mommy?" Janie asked, yawning.

"She's gone downtown with your Aunt Irene," Cherry said. Janie's face started to pucker up. Cherry quickly changed the subject. "Who's ready for a nap?"

"Tell us another story," Betty Lou said.

"Janie, would you like to hear another story?" Cherry asked.

"Yes. I'm sleepy," Janie whispered.

Cherry offered to tell them another story in their own room, while they got ready for their nap. Betty Lou needed persuasion, but she and Janie led Cherry upstairs to their bedroom. There Cherry recounted one of Hans Christian Andersen's wonderful tales, and eventually she got the two children tucked into their beds. They fell asleep.

Cherry sat down on a child's chair, resting, waiting.

A middle-aged woman in an apron came to the door and looked in. "I'm Mattie," she whispered to Cherry. "Isn't Mrs. Belfinger here? And I'm so surprised by those suitcases—"

"Ssh." Cherry joined the houseworker in the hall, closing the children's door, and said softly, "Hello, Mattie. I'm glad you're here. Mrs. Belfinger has gone downtown. She didn't know just when she'd be back. I'm a nurse, I'm Cherry Ames." The woman nodded. "You and I, Mattie, are to stay with Betty Lou and Janie until we hear—hear from their mother," she finished lamely.

Mattie, though she looked mystified, said only, "Well, let's go downstairs, Miss Ames, so as not to disturb the young ones. Betty Lou is a light sleeper."

Downstairs, the maid went about her work without asking Cherry any more questions.

Cherry sat down rather self-consciously in Bunny's lavish living room. She thought over what had happened today, so far. Then, as time dragged on, she read through a newspaper.

Someone knocked lightly. "Didn't want to startle you," Grey said as Cherry looked up.

Bunny was with him. She looked exhausted, dazed, but relieved. "Where are the children?" she asked

Cherry. Then, to Mattie, who came halfway into the hall, "Are they fed? Asleep?"

"Yes, ma'am," Mattie said. "The nurse took care of them."

"Thank you," Bunny said to Cherry. She glanced up at Grey. "May I—? I'd like to go up and see them." When Grey said, "Certainly," Bunny ran up the stairs. Mattie followed her.

Grey called after them, "We're leaving now," but no one answered. He turned to Cherry.

"She'll be allowed to stay with her children," Grey said as he and Cherry walked out of the house. "At least for the time being—she's out on bail. The court allowed her bail because of the children. But Irene's in jail."

"Where she deserves to be," Cherry said. "But what a thing to happen to those children!"

Grey soberly agreed. He looked at his wristwatch. "We have patients to think of. Mr. Goldsmith has lent me his car, so we can drive back promptly to New York. He'll return by train. He has to stay here in Greenhill to handle legal details. But there's no need for us to stay. Come on, Cherry. Back to New York. But first—" Grey lifted her face to his. "I'll have to kiss you later."

"All scratched up, aren't I?"

"It's one of the very best faces, scratches and all," Grey said. "We'll get you fixed up at Brown's Pharmacy and then you owe me a kiss. For bravery."

"Whose bravery?" Cherry asked. "After all, Irene scratched and bit *me*." And she managed to laugh.

CHAPTER XIV

Lady in a Trap

SILENCE — DELAYS — WHO COULD WAIT AND NOT WON-
der? Cherry did her nursing work, and with her Spencer Club friends planned a party. She was working with
Grey at Dr. Fairall's late on Tuesday when the lawyer
telephoned them.

He told them what happened after Cherry and Grey
had left Greenhill. He and a police officer, using the
warrant, had searched Bunny's house. In the closet of
the children's bedroom they found suitcases packed
with their expensive clothes and toys. Bunny and her
sister, Irene Wick Sproull, also had hastily packed two
suitcases apiece full of expensive clothing, furs, jewelry, and perfume. One suitcase was left empty. Irene
Wick admitted it was to have held stolen cash.

Her system of stealing was simple. In her uniform
pocket, at work, she kept cash paid daily by the patients,
and cash rake-offs she received occasionally from Bally

and other favorite suppliers. Mrs. Wick regularly went to the doctors' bank to deposit their patients' checks and cash—as much of the cash as she did not steal. On these bank visits, Mrs. Wick took a few extra minutes to hide the stolen cash in her safe-deposit box. She never put much into her New York bank account where there would be a record of it. In the safe-deposit box there could be no record.

Instead, Mrs. Wick gave large sums of cash at intervals to her sister. Bunny had another name than Wick, lived in another town, and could not readily be connected with Irene. Bunny banked part of the stolen money in a Greenhill savings account in her own name, and she drew extravagantly on it.

Bunny also stashed away still larger sums in a safe-deposit box in the Greenhill bank. This cache was kept there against the dangerous day when Irene might be suspected, and would need to get away fast.

For Irene Wick was a practiced, professional thief. She had worked this racket before, under various names, fleecing doctors in distant parts of the country. She had a police record. Otherwise, all but two times she had managed to escape, just one step ahead of the law, and "disappear." But no matter how large a sum she escaped with, she always went back to her racket. Mrs. Wick, a divorcee, and her widowed, younger sister were greedy for material wealth, and did not care how they got it. Irene Wick was liable, the lawyer said, to several years' imprisonment and a big fine, on charges of felony. Bunny, as her accessory after the fact, was equally liable, for a prison sentence and fine, her children notwithstanding.

The lawyer would eventually succeed in recovering for his three doctor clients the very large sum in Bunny's bank account and in Bunny's safe-deposit box. For now, the money was impounded. This sum did not entirely make up for what Irene Wick had stolen. Mr. Goldsmith expected that when the case went to trial, the court would order the sale of furs, jewelry, and luxury household furnishings that the two women had bought. Proceeds would be returned to the three victimized doctors.

The lawyer reported that Mrs. Wick was surprised that Cherry and Grey had traced her to Greenhill. As secretary she knew, of course, that Dr. Fairall continued to keep on file her "letter of reference" with its Greenhill address. But since the personnel file was confidential, in fact half hidden by medical books, Irene Wick felt fairly safe. At least no one but trusting Dr. Fairall would ever see that faked letter from Greenhill. She never dreamed that Grey and Cherry would look up her reference, much less follow it up with a visit to Greenhill.

Irene Wick brought lump sums of stolen cash to her sister in Greenhill.

She spent many but not all weekends in Greenhill. Once in a while Bunny came to New York to pick up the cash, whenever Irene felt it was growing risky to do so herself. "A cool, professional thief," the lawyer called her. Not so cool now that she was caught—she had developed a facial tic, and actually had cried when arrested.

"I can't feel sorry for her," Cherry said to Grey.

"Look what she did to others," Grey said.

"And I thought she took such a pride in her work," Cherry said wryly. She realized now that Mrs. Wick's touchy, jealous attitudes did not stem from pride—not even from fear of losing her job. No, Irene Wick was bossy and monopolistic because she was guarding, covering up, her stealing from the doctors and virtually stealing from Bally.

"Poor Bally!" Cherry thought about the salesman. "I suppose he needed to make big sales in order to hang on to his job. But imagine paying Mrs. Wick a bribe, a rake-off, an extortion really—in order to get Dr. Fairall's, Dr. Russell's, and Dr. Lamb's supply and medication orders!"

Bally had paid Mrs. Wick part of his sales commission, out of his own pocket.

"It's ugly. Well, at least Bally won't be arrested," Grey answered. "Bally was as much Irene Wick's victim as we three doctors were. He must have needed her large orders very much."

Bally was not the only victim of Mrs. Wick in her role of purchasing agent. The lawyer's investigators had discovered that a pharmacy and a prosthetics manufacturer were paying her cash rake-offs, in return for referring her three doctors' patients to them. It was the pharmacy that had sent the messenger with the blank envelope—filled with cash.

Cherry and Grey both felt badly at how Mrs. Wick had frightened and dominated young Dottie Nash. She had threatened to tell that the young lab technician was a thief. Coming from Mrs. Wick, it was a bad joke! Because she'd caught Dottie borrowing overnight the price of a party dress! The lawyer said that Dottie should be reported to the police. Small sum or not, she had stolen. But Dr. Fairall would not hear of it.

Grey reported that Dr. Fairall was feeling much stronger. He still had to rest at home. Grey and an older doctor who were treating him foresaw a reduced work schedule for Bill Fairall. Fortunately, his book was finished.

"He'll need someone to take Mrs. Wick's place," Cherry said. "Do you think Dr. Fairall would rehire Zelda Colt? I mean if Miss Colt does secretarial work, too? A few nurses do."

Grey smiled at her eagerness. "I thought you'd say that, so I asked Bill Fairall. Told him you believe Irene Wick lied to him about Zelda. I told Dr. Fairall that you had called Zelda in to take your place at the last minute Monday morning. She did beautifully, according to Dr. Lamb."

"Of course, because she cares about doing a good job," Cherry said.

"That's just what Dr. Fairall said. Bill Fairall is going to ask her to come back in case you ever leave, Cherry."

Cherry looked through her eyelashes at Grey. "That may be any minute now, Doctor."

"Stop coquetting and joking with me," Grey said, laughing.

"I'm not entirely joking," Cherry said. "Honestly, Grey. I received a letter from home, with a job offer that's a real surprise to me—"

"You *can't* leave, just when I've gotten used to working with you," Grey said. "Besides, we haven't had that eating contest I once challenged you to."

"Well, if anything could keep me from a fabulous new job, it would be you, Grey dear, and a Kitchen Sink sundae," Cherry said tenderly. She ducked as Grey threw a towel at her.

It was almost time for the party to begin. The Spencer Club nurses felt they owed a party to their friends who had helped with the summer house. Cherry had invited her employers, too. The doctors could use some cheering up after the difficult past week. She hoped Dr. Fairall would be well enough to come, even for a little while. For his convenience mainly, the party was being held in town—a picnic lunch on Saturday noon in Central Park.

Bertha had packed two immense baskets of fried chicken, deviled eggs, bread and butter and tomatoes, fruit and chocolate cake. Josie and Gwen were carrying four lightweight folding chairs that were Grey's contribution—for Dr. Fairall or anyone else needing special consideration. Josie and Gwen earlier had found this peaceful meadow, its boundaries shaded by oak trees. From here, they could hear the tinny music of the children's merry-go-round. The merry-go-round was the guests' meeting place. Cherry stationed herself there, to direct them on to the meadow.

First came those ever-hungry helpers, Spud and Tottie, with the two boys who had helped, too. Cherry welcomed several former patients of the Spencer Club's. So many more friends came that she was pleasantly surprised. Here came their Long Island neighbors, the Peterses, with their small son—they'd come into the city to visit Grandma today, as well. Cherry was delighted to see the Young entourage—led by Henry J., dazzlingly handsome and blond, and carrying the baby. Little H.J. was brown from the sun, and had grown greatly in the country; he gabbled at Cherry.

Leslie smiled at Cherry. "You *did* invite babies to the picnic, too? If not, please tell us." Of course little H.J. was invited, Cherry assured them. Leslie, looking like a ballerina today in a full-skirted pink cotton dress, said Mrs. Faunce and her escort Elijah would be along soon.

Where was Grey? Cherry was beginning to wonder. Almost everyone else was here. Even elderly Dr. Lamb, rakish in a sun hat, had arrived with one of his cronies. Then Cherry saw Grey and Dr. Fairall walking across the grass toward her. Bill Fairall was thin and he did not tear along as usual. But he looked recovered and was smiling. Cherry ran to welcome him.

"Hi, Cherry," he greeted her. "How are you? Grey called for me in a taxi. Glad he did. I wouldn't miss you young ladies' picnic for anything."

"Thank you. And how are you?" Cherry asked.

"Much better," Dr. Fairall said. "Well, some better." Grey smiled and kept silent. Dr. Fairall said, "Grey told me you and he have something more to tell me—and Arnold Goldsmith has, too—about what Irene's been up to."

"Picnic lunch first," said Cherry.

Later, gradually, they told Dr. Fairall the whole story about his trusted employee. They told Dr. Lamb, too, who joined them. Dr. Fairall seemed stunned.

"Well, it's always essential to learn the truth," he said. "I'm indebted to you two."

The Youngs hesitantly came up to them.

"Are we intruding?" Leslie asked for herself and her young husband. "Dr. Fairall, we're so happy to see you here. And we have some good news of our own to tell you. A real triumph for Henry."

With a wife's pride and a showman's flair, Leslie was addressing Dr. Lamb, Grey, and Cherry, too. Henry J. looked embarrassed. He jammed his hands in his pockets, not at all the poised actor. Not in front of Dr. Fairall.

"I think you know, sir, how profoundly grateful I am to you," Henry J. said. "Leslie is, too. Well, Dr. Fairall, I've been lucky enough to win a good role in a play that's opening this fall. The second lead, in fact."

"It's not simply luck," Dr. Fairall said. "I won't embarrass you by saying it's talent, and hard work, and"— Henry J. was perishing of embarrassment—"a lot of other good traits."

Leslie said, "To be practical, and this was *my* idea—" Here Dr. Fairall grinned. "Besides the play, which may not earn a living for us, Henry has landed a bread-and-butter job in television. It pays quite well, it's steady, and it starts *right away*." Leslie gave her husband her I'll-call-you-Julius warning look, and said, "Henry doesn't like the television job very well. I don't blame him. But as long as it doesn't conflict with the play—"

"What we both do like, Dr. Fairall," Henry J. said, not ashamed that others were listening, "is that now we don't have to lean on your generosity. We can pay the rent now at your apartment. And I plan to pay you the rent for the time we lived there—in installments as I earn it, if you'll be patient with me, sir."

Dr. Fairall did not want to accept, but the Youngs insisted, as a matter of self-respect. Otherwise, they said, they would leave the brownstone soon. Irene Wick had already left, in another sense. Possibly Cherry would leave soon, too.

"What a lot of changes!" Cherry said to Grey. "What a lot has happened in that brownstone house!"

"That's partly because," Grey said, "you're the kind of girl things happen to. Or should I say, you're the kind of girl who makes things happen? Or both?"

Cherry started to laugh. "If you'll bring me a peach or some cherries, I might tell you what I plan to do next."

In case you missed *Cherry Ames at Hilton Hospital* ...

CHAPTER 11

Dr. Hope

CHERRY ARRIVED ON THE WARD AHEAD OF TIME THE next morning. Looking into Bob's room, she saw a big, blond man sitting with him. He was Dr. Hope, the head nurse said.

"He's been here for half an hour. Your Bob Smith seems to be talking to him."

"What's Dr. Hope like?" Cherry asked. She had never worked with a psychiatrist, and might not have a chance to do so now. She remembered that psychiatrist, literally, meant a doctor of the soul. "I should think he'd have to have a great deal of sympathy and imagination."

"Well, my friends the Websters live next door to the Hopes," the head nurse said in her practical way, "and they report that Dr. Hope and his two small sons are crackerjack tennis players and that the doctor groans like anyone else when it's his turn to mow the lawn."

Dr. Ray Watson came into the ward, said good morning to the nurses, and waited as anxiously as Cherry. It seemed like a long time until Dr. Hope came out of Bob's room. He looked very thoughtful, but he smiled when he saw Dr. Watson.

"It's not so bad, Ray. The boy is depressed, but he isn't so ill that he can't stay here. I'll recommend that. Of course I'll have our team of psychiatrists come over and examine him—today if they can make it. Personally, I feel hopeful for him."

"That's good, Harry. Glad to hear it."

"Not that we'll have an easy time. There's no guarantee we can help him recover his memory," Dr. Hope said. "But there's a good chance. Now, which is the nurse he talked to?"

Dr. Watson introduced the head nurse and Cherry, and Ruth Dale who was just coming in. Dr. Harry Hope shook hands with all of them and said to Mrs. Peters:

"Can you arrange for Miss Ames to spend extra time with this patient?"

"I'll get an extra nurse's aide, so that she can, Doctor."

Cherry was encouraged to have Dr. Hope accept her, even temporarily, as Bob's nurse. Dr. Ray Watson went with them to a staff office on this floor. There Dr. Hope began a briefing on how they all might best take care of the doubly ill patient.

"First, I think it will be easier for Bob Smith, or whatever his true name is, to have the same nurse—a nurse he already trusts—working along with *both* his medical doctor and with me. . . . Yes, here, Ray. . . . You can count on me to come to Hilton Hospital daily to treat him. He'll make better progress, I think, in your normal hospital surroundings than among our patients who are more seriously disturbed than he is."

Dr. Hope looked with penetration at Cherry. "What did you do to get him to talk?"

"Nothing, Doctor. I spoke softly to him—bathed his feet—that's all."

"Well, you did the right things. He wasn't very willing to talk to me."

"Could it be," Cherry suggested respectfully, "that he finds it harder to talk to a man than a woman—for some key reason?"

Dr. Hope grinned in pleasure and Dr. Watson said, "See, I told you she catches on fast."

Cherry felt pleased and embarrassed, and later fascinated by what Dr. Hope went on to say.

An amnesic like Bob Smith had thousands of fellow wanderers. Mental health authorities in all states were doing everything possible to help them and send them home. In past centuries they, and those with more serious mental illness, had been ignorantly regarded as willfully dangerous or evil, and thrown into dungeons and chained as criminals. This practice dated back to the Middle Ages when people believed that "demons" had "taken possession" of these unhappy persons. Now, Dr. Hope said, although the medical profession and the law recognized that a few psychotics might do dangerous or criminal acts, and must be restrained, the mentally ill were treated as any other sick persons and given medical care. He added that their suffering was bewildering and intense, perhaps harder to bear than the pain of physical illness. Nowadays, though, with good care, very many became well and happy and sound citizens again.

"About Bob Smith—"

Dr. Hope said that he was—unconsciously— forgetting certain *carefully selected* things in his past, things that he found impossible to face. These were the very things that he must be helped to remember, and to face and deal with. Dr. Hope's job would be a sort of detective work, to find these forgotten facts in Bob's clouded memory. To do this, he would use various uncovering techniques.

Dr. Ray Watson asked loudly the same thing Cherry was thinking. "Talking about detective work, why don't we call on the Hilton police force and see if they can help us? Of course they already know about the motorist's report, and they know we have an unidentified man here as a fracture case. But we haven't yet told the police this is an amnesia victim."

Dr. Hope hesitated. "Asking police help doesn't always work out. These amnesia cases can be surprisingly difficult. The clues and secrets are locked away inside the person. Making them ill, you see. However, we'll give the police a try, Ray."

"Bob probably will be able to remember unimportant things," Dr. Hope said. "It will be a start, at least. Miss Ames, I wish you'd carefully examine his clothes or belongings for any—what would the police call it, Ray?"

"Any identifying feature, I guess."

"Yes, I will, Dr. Hope," said Cherry.

She returned to Orthopedics, tiptoed into Bob Smith's room, and softly closed the door behind her. Her patient was dozing. Bob must have slept off his first exhaustion, for his thin face was a more normal color than it had been yesterday. But his breathing was rapid and shallow, and his hands twitched in his sleep, and he frowned.

"Nervous and upset even in his sleep," Cherry thought. She glanced at the chart and the night nurse's report: temperature normal, pulse 90 per minute, complained of headache; his movements were abnormally slow, a symptom of depressed feelings. Well, on his breakfast tray the teacup and plate were emptied; that was one good thing.

In the closet Cherry found Bob Smith's shabby garments and systematically searched them. No labels, no dry cleaner's tags, nothing in the trousers pockets. No leads, in short. In a jacket pocket, she found a small calendar for this year. Its pages were torn off up to April.

"April! This is September. Did time stop for Bob in April? Was it April when his memory blacked out? If so, where had he been in the six months since that date?"

Cherry tried the jacket's other pockets. . . . Empty . . . another empty . . . wait, there was something in the inside pocket. She pulled out a piece of thin white paper. A letter. There was no envelope, hence no postmark, and the letter bore no date. It was in a feminine handwriting, without a salutation, and was signed "S." It read:

"It was good of you to tell me what you did last evening. At the moment I didn't understand you. I hadn't realized that he's under such a handicap. Now I do and I *will* make allowances. So don't worry. S."

Cherry read the note again. It hinted at more than it said. Who was "S" and who was "he"? She suddenly felt Bob Smith looking at her. She was startled but maintained her calm.

"Hello. How do you feel this morning?"

Didn't he recognize her? He seemed to be in a hazy, dreamy state.

"Bob, I'm looking in your pockets for something to identify you. We're trying here at the hospital to help you."

He said weakly, "I know."

Good! He did recognize her! He did understand. Cherry thought of things to say to him—about bringing him back to the present, about sending him home. Better not. Maybe Bob Smith did not want to go home—or maybe he had no home. She could stir up a storm of emotions in him with a few wrong words. Talking, or forcing Bob to talk, could be as disastrous as giving a patient the wrong medicine. Better wait for Dr. Hope to lead the way.

"Bob, may I keep this note and the calendar?"

No answer. She took his silence for assent.

During the morning, Cherry made Bob comfortable, and applied cold compresses for his headache. Presently Miss Bond, a new employee in the Admitting Office, came in. She carried a ledger. She had been advised, evidently, to conduct the interview with Bob Smith through the nurse. He listened but would not speak.

"Can you give me the usual information?" Miss Bond asked crisply. "Name, age, address, occupation, names of any relatives?"

"I—I don't think that's available at the moment. Bob?" Cherry glanced at him. He looked away, dazed. Cherry shook her head at Miss Bond.

"Can you tell me," Miss Bond continued, "how and where the patient got hurt? Any previous illnesses? Shall we list him temporarily as John Doe?"

Cherry saw tears well up in her patient's eyes. He pulled the covers around him as if trying to hide. Cherry went to sit beside him and said:

"Miss Bond, will you excuse us now? We'll send the information to the Admitting Office as soon as we can."

"Well, it's most unusual—Oh, I see. Yes, surely, Nurse." Miss Bond left, red in the face with embarrassment.

For a few minutes Cherry held Bob Smith's hand in silence. Then he turned his head so that he could look at her.

"I'm sorry. All mixed up. I'm so ashamed."

"Don't be. It's all right."

"I can't even remember my own name. It's terrifying."

"S-sh, now. You'll remember."

Cherry waited. His breathing grew less agitated, more regular.

"Nurse? Miss—Miss Cherry?"

"That's right."

"I think I've been using the name of Bob Smith. I made it up. It sounded like a real name to me."

Cherry nodded and kept silent. His hand in hers relaxed, and then he fell asleep. She felt immensely sorry for this young man. Never had she seen anyone so lost and alone.

At lunchtime Mrs. Ball, who headed the hospital's Social Service Department, rapped and asked Cherry whether it would be advisable for her to see Bob Smith. Cherry hesitated about another interview. But she knew Leona Ball to be perceptive and kind, so Cherry said:

"Well, Mrs. Ball, come in but just say hello."

Mrs. Ball took a long look at the dazed man.

"No, I see I'd better not. Let me know what I can do for him—perhaps I could contact public or private agencies, or send out inquiries about him?"

"That would be a great help."

One further, long interview did take place that afternoon. The team of psychiatrists came, as Dr. Hope had promised, to give Bob a further examination, and see to what extent they agreed with Dr. Hope's first findings. Cherry was not present; she did her regular work on Orthopedics. After three o'clock, when the psychiatric team had gone, Dr. Hope called her into the staff office. He talked to Cherry privately.

"Well, it's agreed Bob is to stay at Hilton Hospital. Sit down, Miss Ames. Here's what happened in consultation this afternoon, so you'll have a clearer picture of our patient, and what you and I are going to do for Bob."

Cherry sat down, all attention. She watched this big, vigorous man pace around the office, stand still to think, pace, and then grin at her.

"Now isn't it reasonable for me to be disappointed that we can't interview Bob Smith's relatives? Relatives could fill in his life history, and tell us all sorts of relevant things. We always talk to the family first thing on admitting a patient—but with Bob, we don't even know if he's got a family. But we did take certain tests, and we'll do more."

The team of psychiatrists had given Bob, so far as his illness permitted today, a psychometric test that measured intelligence and the Rorschach "ink blot" test. The latter helped bring out ideas that troubled him, but only in a very general way. Later on, the team might take an encephalogram or brain-wave photograph. So far, the psychiatrists were satisfied that "Bob Smith" had sustained no brain injury or disease, had better than average intelligence, and had lost his memory because of some severe psychological upset. Exactly what had happened to Bob to cause this, and exactly how to treat Bob, was up to Dr. Hope to discover.

"We'll have to feel our way, at first," Dr. Hope said.

"We, Doctor?"

"Certainly. You're Bob's nurse and my assistant."

"But I'm not especially trained for this kind of case, you know," said Cherry. "I had one course at nursing school, of course—"

"The patient trusts you. You have imagination. That could be enough. At least I'm going to try you out."

Dr. Hope bent down and peered at Cherry.

"What's that worried look about? See here, better than fifty-five percent of so-called mental cases are temporary. After we help them analyze their problems and give them a few days' 'first aid,' they come to themselves and can go home." He laughed. "One man was brought in to our Mental Hygiene Clinic because he was standing on a street corner distributing dollar bills. Well, he was celebrating winning the sweepstakes, and he was always a generous man."

Cherry smiled, too. "I guess a sense of humor is going to come in handy."

"Not that Bob Smith is as mild a case as these. Yes, we'll need humor, and kindness, and a hopeful outlook. We must listen compassionately to whatever Bob says, and not pass judgment on him but try to understand. You and I will have to do our very best for him. We're the only people he has to help him."

"And he has me. I care about him, too." Dr. Ray Watson stood in the doorway. "Hope, do you intend to work at the University Hospital or at this hospital—or both?"

"Both," Dr. Hope said cheerfully. "This young nurse is going to do double duty, too."

Dr. Watson mumbled something about "Hard work and idealism never hurt anybody—only way to cure the patients." Then he said:

"By the way, I asked Leona Ball to telephone the police department. They're sending one of their detectives. Name of Hal Treadway. He'll be here tomorrow to talk to our mystery patient."

"Well, Miss Cherry," said Dr. Hope, "when you see the right moment, you'd better tell Bob that a visitor is coming to help him. Prepare him."

"I'll try, Dr. Hope."

CHAPTER III

First Steps

THE DETECTIVE'S FORMAL QUESTIONING ON FRIDAY distressed Bob Smith and yielded no information. That was not the detective's fault. Hal Treadway was an unobtrusive little man in sports clothes, perfectly agreeable to have Cherry and Dr. Hope in the room while he asked his questions. But Bob grew irritable. He broke out into a sweat and stammered:

"I don't know where I got the money to leave my hometown. Or anything! If I could remember I'd tell you."

"Take it easy, son," said the detective. "Try and think where your folks are. Where's your mother? Can you tell me *her* name?"

"I don't know! I mean, I haven't any family." Bob pulled himself up by the hand straps and sat bolt upright in bed. He was shaky and indignant. "If I had a family, wouldn't they be looking for me?"

"Not necessarily," the detective muttered, but Dr. Hope stood up to put an end to the interview.

"Sorry, Mr. Treadway, the patient can't tolerate any more direct questioning. We can't press him. Will you come into the hall with me? Nurse—" Dr. Hope indicated the enamel tray with its plain tepid water and sponge. "Take care of Bob, then join us, please."

"Yes, Dr. Hope."

Left alone with her patient, Cherry gently put cold applications on his burning forehead. She gave Bob another healing dose of silence and he quieted down. His eyes followed her as she lowered the window shades, then came back to the bed and turned his pillows over to the cool, fresher side.

"Miss Cherry? I guess you think I don't want to cooperate."

He sounded anxious. She reassured him.

"You see, Miss Cherry, I realize I'm in an odd condition. I've realized it for a long time. Though I don't know how long." Bob's brows wrinkled in his effort to grasp time. "Anyhow, all the time I was wandering and working at odd jobs—"

Wandering. Working at odd jobs. Cherry filed these bits of information away in her mind. These were the first leads Bob had mentioned.

"—I was afraid to talk to other people. Afraid they'd see how odd I am at present, and commit me to an insane asylum. I'm not insane." He looked at her pleadingly. "Am I?"

"No, Dr. Hope doesn't think so. The other doctors don't think so. You're ill, and you'll get well."

"I feel so alone."

Cherry took both the patient's hands in hers. "You're not alone. I care, and Dr. Hope cares, and Dr. Watson cares very much about you. We're going to give you our very best, skilled medical care. If you'll just trust us and work with us—"

"I will." Bob cleaned back and closed his eyes. "You're nice."

Cherry left him to drift off to sleep. She rejoined Dr. Hope and the detective in the hospital corridor. Dr. Hope was explaining to Mr. Treadway that contact with the police would only aggravate Bob's emotional upset, which accompanied and caused his amnesia.

"Don't you think, sir," the detective asked, "that if this boy doesn't like talking to the police, there might be a good reason for it? Apart from his—ah—state of mind, that is. How do you know he isn't mixed up in some crime?"

"We don't know," Dr. Hope said. "It's possible. Anything is possible, with an unknown person. But as I told you—"

"All right, Doctor, I'll work with Bob only through you and the nurse. I'll start right away to try to trace his identity and connections."

Cherry was curious about what methods Hal Treadway would use. Dr. Hope was curious, too.

"Well, while I'll certainly do all I can," the police detective said, "you have to understand what's involved in a case like your patient's."

In order to locate a missing person, or to identify a haggard, undoubtedly changed wanderer like Bob, required the cooperation of large numbers of police experts, long periods of time, long distances of travel, and often the almost endless study of great numbers of records.

"We have urgent cases like Bob Smith's turn up oftener than you'd think," the detective said. "But we're the Hilton police, and our first attention has to go to local cases and Hilton people. Unfortunately we haven't enough men, nor enough time and expense money, to conduct a detailed investigation on *every* missing persons case."

In Bob's case, Detective Treadway explained, he had no identifying features or scars as clues. He was just a nice-looking young man. At present he was so thin, wind-burned, and shaggy that he probably was hardly recognizable. As for the letter and calendar Cherry had found in his pocket, they revealed next to nothing. His blistered feet told rather more.

"From past experiences with these cases," the detective said, "I'd conjecture that Bob has kept moving."

"Kept moving," Dr. Hope repeated. "Of course that doesn't tell us whether he's wandered a long way from his home, or whether he kept moving within a limited area."

"The chances are that he comes from some distant part of the United States," Hal Treadway said. "Something inside them drives these wanderers."

The police detective promised to send out a teletype description on Bob to the police of other cities; to list him with the nationwide Missing Persons Bureau; to check his fingerprints with large agencies like Army, passport bureau, big employers, and civil service—at once.

"It'll take time for these people to check their files, though."

"Time!" Dr. Hope made an impatient gesture. "We can't afford to wait around. The patient could grow worse. This young man won't get well unless and until he can be helped to learn who he is. Then he'll have to remember what forgotten situation is troubling him. Otherwise—no cure."

Dr. Hope's warning registered with Cherry.

"We *can't* wait, Mr. Treadway!"

"Well, Doctor," the detective said, "I'll take Bob's clothing and try to find out, personally, whether it has any identifying marks, and if so, check these leads."

Cherry ventured to say that she had examined Bob's garments and found no markings or labels.

Hal Treadway told her, "There could be markings not visible to the naked eye. I'll examine Bob's clothing under our ultraviolet bulb. It's a violation of the law for a laundry or dry cleaning establishment not to mark garments, and I've never seen a worn garment yet that wasn't marked. When we hold Bob's jacket under the blue bulb, the chances are we'll see a series of numbers and symbols. Then I'll check those with the Laundry and Dry Cleaner Mark Identification Bureau, which has national coverage."

"Then there's some chance of immediate information?" Dr. Hope asked.

"If we're lucky. I'll check also with all local employers who hire transient help."

Cherry brought Bob Smith's garments for the police detective to take with him. He promised to get in touch with the hospital people as soon as he discovered anything. Dr. Hope thanked him, but after the detective left, remarked to Cherry:

"The police procedures are going to take time, and it looks as if he can make only a limited investigation. I'm not satisfied. Are you, Miss Cherry?"

It surprised her to have this doctor turn to her so informally and ask her opinion. Still, she was a member of his medical team and he seemed to want to talk over with her anything that affected their patient.

"I should think all we can do," Cherry answered, "is wait and see what the detective can accomplish."

"Bob can't wait too long. I think we'll try our first Pentothal interview with him tomorrow."

Cherry knew that Pentothal was a drug, to be administered by physicians, preferably in hospitals, and that Dr. Hope intended to use it as an uncovering technique. He explained exactly how and why.

Whatever had happened to Bob, he resisted remembering it. Pentothal would relax him and help ease his fear of what happened—or what he feared was going to happen. Once relaxed, he would be able to break through his amnesia and recall a few facts about himself. Or so Dr. Hope expected.

"We'll have to be very easy and tactful with him," Dr. Hope told Cherry. "If we press him too hard, we'll only frighten him and he won't talk to us."

Cherry nodded. "Will you explain to him first what we're going to try to do?"

"Yes. And we'll tell Bob that we're making a record of what he says, and why."

Since there were going to be several interviews, Dr. Hope would need a record so that he could review details and, later on, grasp the picture of Bob's life as a whole. Bob's memories would emerge in a confused manner, Dr. Hope predicted, because Bob himself was ill and disorganized. Dr. Hope and Cherry would have to piece the bits together into some sort of meaning. In order to keep records, they would place a microphone in Bob's room; this would be piped to a tape recorder in the next room or in the closet. They would tell Bob about the microphone, and also tell him they would conceal it, so that the constant sight of it would not make him self-conscious and inhibit his talking.

Cherry was intrigued. This promised to be the strangest kind of sleuthing she had ever done—pursuing a man's forgotten memories of his past—and she commented on it.

"We'll have to explore two kinds of past with Bob," said Dr. Hope. "One is his *recent* past, because some recent shock or crisis or facing an impossible situation has brought on his amnesia. But a sound person can face a crisis and not go to pieces. It's fair to assume that in some

respect Bob has a psychological weak spot or injury—
and has had it for a long time. It probably goes far back to
some deep-seated distress in his childhood. So we'll also
try to help him remember into his *far* past."

"That will make our puzzle all the harder to piece
together," Cherry said.

"Yes." Dr. Hope smiled at her.

"And when we do bring his troubles to light? What
then?"

"*If* and when," Dr. Hope corrected her. "Then we'll
have to help him face his troubles. Sometimes it's a
question of straightening out mistaken ideas a patient
has. Sometimes it's a matter of supportive treatment,
giving the patient reassurance and strength to meet
some difficult situation. Or sometimes, many times,
the practitioner must do both."

"I—I'm not experienced enough for this case,"
Cherry said.

"Try," Dr. Hope said. "If it doesn't work out, I'll have a
psychiatric nurse from my own hospital work with me.
But I think you'll do fine."

Dr. Hope, of course, would take the lead with Bob,
and that would guide her. Even so, the delicacy and
complexity of the treatment left Cherry with some
qualms. In comparison, she found that the physical
nursing that Dr. Watson had ordered was simple.

For the broken leg, all they could do these first few
days was wait and make careful observations. In order
to be sure the cast was not too tight, so that it interfered
with the circulation and caused swelling, Cherry felt

her patient's toes to see if they were warm or cold. She frequently examined the edges of the cast and skin for pressure points and irritation. The cast itself was supported by pillows to keep the bones in alignment; pillows also provided Bob with other support. Cherry and the orderly helped him to change his position often; he had a light cast so that he could be moved and turned. This was important, for if the patient did not move or was afraid to turn, immobility could lead to slowing of his digestive processes, loss of appetite, bedsores, even some risk of pneumonia. Although Bob needed extended bed rest, Cherry knew how important it was to encourage him to turn and move, and to eat.

Bob's chart showed he was anemic, and he was a little irritable. But already he was improving, less exhausted, less panicky, after three days' bed rest and treatment. If only his sleep were not so restless, as the night nurse reported. . . . Cherry did not neglect her other patients, but her mind was on Bob.

When she came on duty the next morning, she found Bob Smith just waking up. He was cheerful and even whistled a little. She hoped that augured well for the Pentothal interview. Mrs. Peters suggested, "Leave his door open, so that he can see the other people on our ward." Cherry did so, and moved his bed so that he could look out. Bob watched with mild interest; elderly Mr. Pape and Tommy waved to him. But after half an hour his eyes took on that glazed, faraway stare again. Cherry closed the door. Well, he'd seen the ward and that was a start.

"Who's that young fellow with the broken leg?" the other patients asked. "Why is he in there?"

"Sure, move him in with the rest of us busted bones," Tommy said. "Everybody gets homesick in a hospital."

Mrs. Peters explained that Bob Smith had had a bad shock, and needed to be quiet and in a private room for a while. She, Ruth Dale, and the orderly knew more than that about his illness. There was no need for the patients to know, however; they might misunderstand. Dr. Hope wanted the other men to treat Bob naturally and easily, if he improved enough to be brought on the ward. Normal companionship could be part of his cure. If and when he came out of his long silences—if today's first uncovering technique would work—

That afternoon Dr. Hope went alone into Bob's room. Cherry presumed he talked to Bob, to prepare him for the interview, and administered the Pentothal. After an interval, Dr. Hope summoned Cherry.

She went into Bob's half-darkened room where a softly lighted lamp burned at his bedside. It was quiet, almost hushed, in here. Bob appeared to be more relaxed than she had yet seen him. His face was flushed and the pupils of his eyes were dilated, but he smiled at Cherry.

"Hello, Miss Cherry. I'm going to do my best."

"I'm sure you are."

She sat down in the chair beside Dr. Hope's, as he indicated, next to the bed.

"Would you like a cool drink, Bob? Chewing gum?" Dr. Hope offered them.

"No, thank you. I'm not thirsty. I just had a cool—" His voice trailed off.

"Just relax, Bob." Dr. Hope nodded and leaned back in his chair. He was unhurried. "You must have had a hard time. Can you tell Miss Cherry and me where you were just a few days ago?"

"I guess it was around here."

"Mmmm. What did the place look like?"

"Trees. Streets. People. No one I knew." Bob broke into a sweat. "Can *you* tell me what town this is? Hilton, I think you said, but what state?"

"Illinois." Dr. Hope answered as if Bob's question were a perfectly natural one. "Have you ever been in Illinois before?"

"Not that I know of."

"When I say *home* to you, what do you think of? Close your eyes and think. Take your time."

Bob made an effort. "A large white frame house," he said vaguely.

"I suppose that's where your family lives."

"I have no family!"

Dr. Hope nudged Cherry. She said pleasantly, hoping it was the right cue:

"Everyone has a family."

"Well, I haven't. I—I'm the sole survivor."

Cherry was inclined to believe him, but she saw a tiny frown between Dr. Hope's eyes. He said:

"Haven't you anyone at all? Who were your family members?"

"No one—no one—"

"Your father," Dr. Hope prompted. No answer. "And your mother. Where is your mother?"

Bob grew so distressed that Dr. Hope said:

"Never mind. Let it go for now. Unless you want to tell us why you believe you're the sole survivor?"

"I—My father is dead."

"Yes. How long ago?"

"While I was still in school. In college."

"I see. By the way, which college did you attend?"

Bob turned his face away. A minute went by. "I can't remember," he said painfully.

Dr. Hope said that was all right, he would remember everything in good time.

"And your mother?"

"She's dead, I tell you! How many times must I say so—I beg your pardon. Very rude of me."

Bob's excitement about his mother—he had replied calmly about his father—was not lost on either Dr. Hope or Cherry. Cherry smoothed over the bad moment by offering Bob a drink of water. He was glad of the lull. Dr. Hope resumed:

"Well, let's see now, Bob Smith. That isn't really your name, is it?"

"No, I made it up when I was in a town—around here, I think—and I was applying for an odd job in a—possibly a restaurant? The man in charge asked my name and—"

Dr. Hope nodded. "What is your name?"

Bob forced a grin. "I'd like to know that myself." For that much humor and courage, Cherry patted his hand.

"Miss Cherry?" said Dr. Hope. "You have a brother, I hear," and gave her the lead.

"Yes, a twin brother, in fact." She tried to think what events in her brother Charlie's life might be paralleled in any young man's life. "He's seen service in the Air Force. Have you been in the armed forces, Bob?"

"No, I haven't." He seemed entirely calm and certain about this.

"But you're the right age for it," Cherry said.

"Yes, but I haven't. I know when I was in my teens I went to a boys' summer camp and they taught us how to handle rifles—marksmanship—we had a shooting range—and I know that I attended college, because I remember the long quiet hours of study. But I haven't been in any of the armed services," he said very definitely.

This seemed unlikely to Cherry. She glanced at Dr. Hope for his reaction, but his expression was noncommittal, friendly.

"You're about twenty-five, I'd say, aren't you, Bob?"

"Twenty-six, I think, sir, if I've got the present year right."

Cherry told him the year, matter-of-factly, as if she were telling him the hour. Poor Bob was lost in time.

"Thank you," he said. "I wish I knew what date it was when I left home."

Cherry remembered the calendar she had found in his pocket, with the paper torn off at last April. She had better not mention it unless Dr. Hope did so. He chose instead to pick up another thread of Bob's remark.

"When you left home, you say. That was the large white house. Picture the house in your mind's eye, Bob, and tell me what feelings it stirs up in you."

Bob threw his arm across his eyes, and thought. When he took his arm away, he looked bewildered.

"I *know* there is something I should be worried about, but I can't remember what it is."

"You *know*? How do you know?"

"I just do. I'm sure of it. It troubles me."

"*It*?"

Bob said sadly, "I only know that I do—or rather, I ought to feel terribly worried and responsible."

"Some trouble about your family," Cherry murmured. "With the large white house."

"No."

"With what place, then?" Dr. Hope asked.

Bob sank back, tired. "I don't know. It just doesn't come clear to me. I almost see some place to tell you about, and then it's as if a wall of mist rises up."

"All right, you've done fine." The doctor signaled to Cherry that the drug was wearing off. "A good start. See if you can't take a nap now, Bob."

He was already dozing off.

Cherry tiptoed out after Dr. Hope. They held a brief conference in the hall. Dr. Hope held up one hand and counted off on his fingers what this first interview had yielded.

"First, Bob denies he has a family, but he recalls a white house and grows upset at mention of his mother. Very cloudy there. Second, he says he's been to college.

I'm inclined to believe that; he talks like an educated man. Maybe he'll remember or describe what college, and we can trace his identity through college records. Third, he's sure he never had military service, but can't explain why not. Yet he's the right age and physically fit. He probably was balanced enough until some unbearable stress caused this breakdown—"

Dr. Hope was inclined to believe Bob had had some military service but was actively forgetting it. Cherry reminded him that the detective, who had fingerprinted Bob, would check on that.

"Good. What else? Bob said he *knew* that he *ought* to feel concerned and responsible about something. And that 'something' is the crux of his present difficulty."

"Present difficulty—an injury rooted probably in his childhood?" Cherry asked, "Did I notice correctly that Bob remembered only the recent past in this interview? Didn't remember his far past at all?"

"Right! Bob remembered that he'd had odd jobs around here. As we'd expect. Now, if we or that detective fellow could locate his employers—"

Cherry made a suggestion, and Dr. Hope approved it. Their uncharted search was under way.

In case you missed *Cherry Ames, Island Nurse* ...

~~~~~~

CHAPTER II

The Three from the Plane

WITHIN A VERY SHORT TIME, CHERRY HAD THE BEDROOM of the suite ready for the patient and everything prepared according to Dr. Joe's instructions. But just to be sure, she stood for a moment in the middle of the room to check again.

Near the head of the bed were the two intravenous stands—"IV" stands the nurses called them—which a hospital attendant had brought from the supply room where such equipment was kept for use as required. From one stand hung the pint container of normal saline, a lifesaving salt solution that would likely be infused into a patient's vein. The other stand would hold a pint of blood for transfusion after the patient's blood had been typed for compatibility.

"The man had a sudden hemorrhage and lost a lot of blood," Dr. Fortune had told Cherry over the phone. "He'll need a transfusion."

She also had ready an oxygen tank and mask, thermometer, cotton swabs, adhesive tape, bottles of antiseptic and anesthetic, sterile gauze pads, needles and tubing used in giving intravenous treatment, hypodermic needles, and other medical supplies.

Everything had been done that could be done beforehand. The bedroom had become a little hospital within a hospital. Cherry gave a nod of satisfaction and looked at her watch. The ambulance should be back from the airfield at any minute.

She had already alerted the laboratory to have someone ready to test the patient's blood. Now, she heard a knock at the door and a voice call "Miss Ames," and Millie Reynolds, one of the laboratory technicians, came bustling in.

"They have *all* arrived. I saw them bring in the patient, so I didn't have to wait for your call," she announced. Millie was a blond, blue-eyed girl who looked as if she could not possibly have a brain in her head, but she was one of the best laboratory technicians at Hilton.

Cherry had noticed the accent on "all" and she smiled. "How many exactly, Millie, are there with the patient?" she asked. "You make it sound as if he were royalty accompanied by his entourage."

"Well, it's practically that," Millie said. "I heard this big, handsome hunk of man say something about his uncle, Sir Something-or-other, that's the patient. ... Imagine a patient with a title! Isn't it exciting?"

Millie did not have time to tell about "the others" with the sick man, for there were sounds of movement in the hall and a hospital attendant rolled in a still form. He was followed by Dr. Fortune and two young men, one of them in pilot's uniform, his visored hat in his hand.

Dr. Joe gave Cherry one of his warm smiles, then glanced at Millie.

"Doctor, Miss Reynolds is ready to check the blood at once," Cherry explained.

"Very good." Turning to the two young men, Dr. Joe told them, "You may wait here in the sitting room."

The patient was taken into the bedroom and the door closed. Things must be done quickly. There was no time to waste; a man's life was threatened. In the next instant, the three of them—Dr. Joe, Millie, and Cherry—became an efficient team.

The man was unconscious. His flesh was gray and clammy from loss of blood and shock. His pulse was rapid.

The mask was placed over his face and the flow of oxygen regulated.

The rubber bands and tubing for the IV administration were adjusted. Cherry wiped a spot over the veins of one arm with a swab of cotton soaked in antiseptic. The doctor injected a small amount of a local anesthetic to numb the arm slightly, then deftly pushed the hollow needle into a vein in the bend of the patient's elbow, and the slow drip of liquid into the vein began.

Meanwhile, Millie had quickly pricked a finger and drawn a little of the man's blood into a tiny vial. Off she went with it to the laboratory, where she would test it immediately for blood type. The transfusion could not be given until this was known.

Aided by Cherry, Dr. Joe proceeded with the examination of his patient.

At the airfield and during the ride in the ambulance, the nephew and the pilot had told the doctor what had happened. And between listening through his stethoscope, checking of pulse and breathing, gently feeling the patient's stomach and abdomen, Dr. Joe gave Cherry bits and pieces of information.

"Fellow collapsed in a plane not far from here. ... Name's Barclay—Sir Ian Barclay. ... Haven't seen him in ten years. ... Owns iron mines up in Canada. ... Peptic-ulcer case. ... Nephew said doctor up there had been treating him for some time. ... Lloyd Barclay, that's the nephew's name, said his uncle was getting along pretty well ... then this sudden hemorrhage. ... Uncle went to make telephone call to check on how things were going in his mines. ... Found there was trouble. ... Sudden anxiety probably set off this attack."

The door opened. Dr. Joe's and Cherry's heads turned as one to Millie, with a bottle from the hospital's blood bank in her hands.

"Group O, Rhesus positive," she told them, "and the patient's is the same—perfect match." She walked briskly over with it, then as briskly out again.

Group O was a common blood type and could be safely given to anyone belonging to the other main groups—A, B, or Ab—just as long as the Rhesus— or RH—factor was the same. That Sir Ian Barclay's belonged to this common type was certainly a bit of good luck right at the start, Cherry thought, as she swabbed his arm with a bit of antiseptic-soaked cotton in preparation for the transfusion.

Cherry and Dr. Joe could only wait now while the science of medicine, which had taken man many centuries to develop, took over. Sir Ian's body must be supplied with oxygen, so he breathed it into his lungs through the snoutlike device invented for the purpose. The salt and liquid his body had lost were being replaced by the saline. And lifegiving blood flowed into his veins from the bottle hanging from the stand.

Sir Ian Barclay was breathing easily now. Some of the grayness had given way to the faint violet of returning blood. His flesh was warmer and drier.

Familiar as she was with the care and healing of the sick, Cherry never ceased to wonder at the miracle of medicine. And one was taking place before her eyes right now.

It was true that there were failures, and there was so very much yet unknown about health and sickness—yet what science and good care could do was no less a miracle. Perhaps that was why it was the most important thing in the world to her to be a nurse, Cherry thought. She was a part of the wonder of healing.

That was the way Dr. Joe had always felt too. He had given his whole life to medicine. A small, friendly man who spoke slowly and haltingly—who would think of him as a hero? He was a modern-day hero, nevertheless.

She saw Dr. Joe put his hand on Sir Ian's forehead. Then he listened again to the patient's heartbeat.

"Looks as if we'll bring him through," Dr. Joe said, straightening up.

He pulled up a chair beside the bed and nodded to one near Cherry. "Might as well sit as stand at this point," he said.

They sat in silence. Cherry knew that Dr. Joe would add nothing to what he had told her before. That much information he had given her because she needed to be oriented to the case. Sir Ian Barclay at the moment was not a personality to the doctor, but a sick human being who must be made well again.

As Cherry sat beside Sir Ian, the lean, powerful figure, with its strong, bony face and gray-streaked black hair, began to pique her curiosity. "Here is a man," she thought, "who looks as if he had great strength of character. He is a wealthy mine owner. A Canadian with a title. He is on a tour of mines in the United States. He calls home, hears bad news, collapses shortly afterward."

"Sudden hemorrhage of a peptic ulcer," Dr. Joe had said. People with ulcers had sudden flare-ups—that Cherry knew. Bad news could cause an attack. What had been the nature of the bad news that had caused this wealthy man, with the sturdy look of an eagle, to collapse, she wondered.

A mumbling came suddenly from the bed.

Both Cherry and Dr. Joe jumped.

Sir Ian Barclay had opened his gray eyes and was staring at them.